ATROPA BELLADONNA

THE FALLEN ANGELS OF THE EAST END

JACKSON COLE, JR.

DARK SUNS
PUBLISHING

Published by
Darksuns LLC
P.O. Box 278
Wading River, NY 11792

Cover art and design by Jackson Cole Jr.

ISBN: 979-8-9886488-0-2

The busy bee has no time for sorrow.
—William Blake

PART I

ABOUT A GIRL

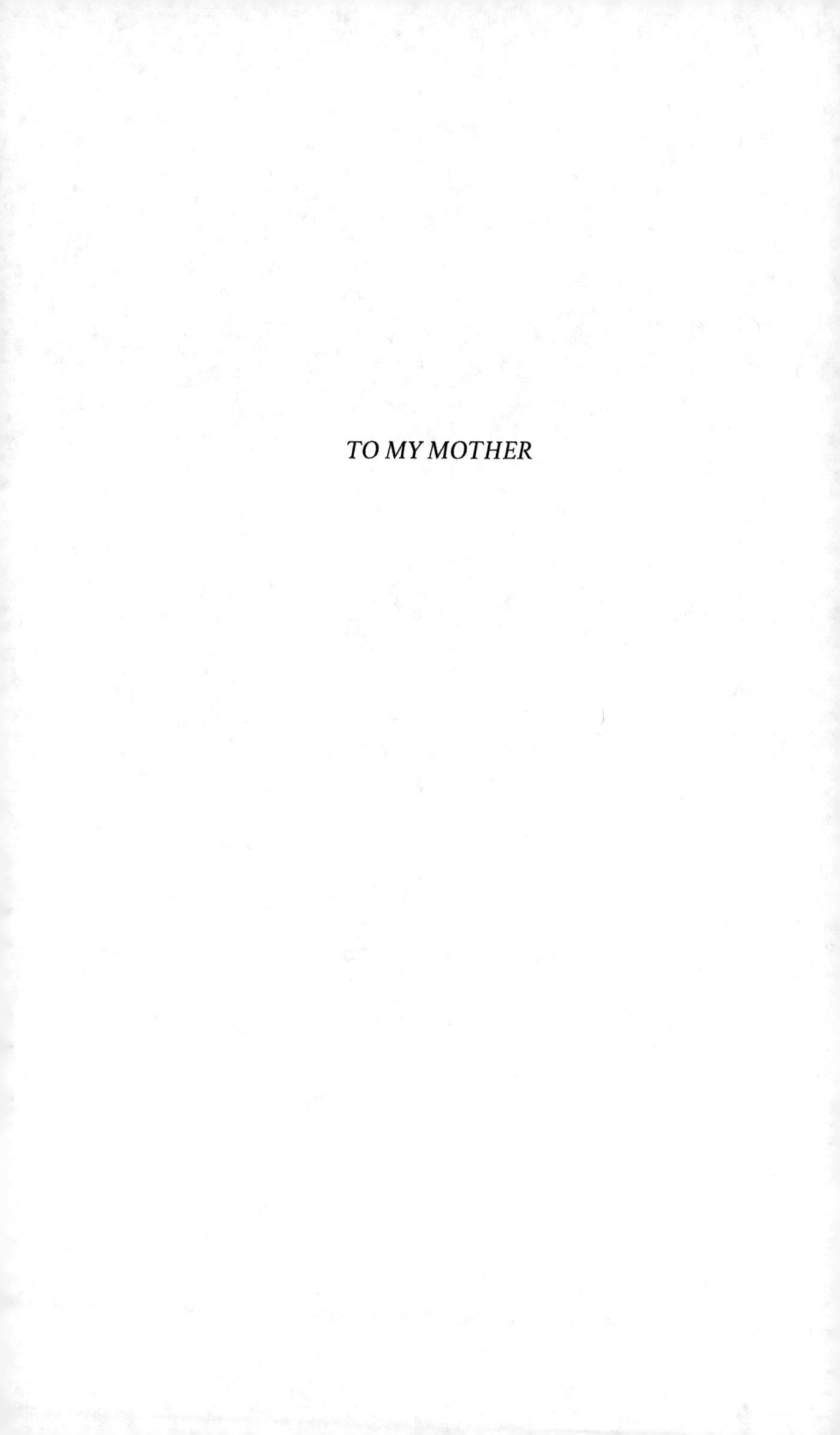

TO MY MOTHER

MY BODY PARTS

0

AND HE WILL STAY WHERE HIS HEART PLEASES....

And he closes his eyes, wishing he was in there with her again. And it happens. He's there. Beside her. Sitting on the edge of her bed as she lay in the fetal position, facing the wall, covered by her favorite pink fuzzy blanket. He strokes the top of her bleached white hairs that poke out the top of the blanket. He is frightened as his hand trembles. Eyes gleaming. Pupils widening. He senses something and turns toward the door. The quick footsteps thundering down the hall, trotting closer...he gets to his feet and backs up, backs up, BACKS UP! across the room, feeling for the dresser and props himself up in one motion, reaching for the window as there's a knock-knock! And opening the door in one motion — Lemme guess. Again, ya sick?! He is already on the other side of the window looking in as if he never entered in the first place.

1

FEBRUARY, 1995

Her stomach hurts again. Shelly crunches herself into a ball and rolls to her left side. If she misses school once more, she's probably not gonna graduate on time. Four months, four months, only four months left. Keep sayin' it ta ya self ya lazy bitch. Now get up. Ya can do this. Anything it takes to get out of this shithole by June. She turns over on her stomach and stretches her legs. The bed is too soft and warm to get up. A sudden wave of shivers comes over her body. She hates it when the cold air hits her skin, making it like every hair on her arms and legs is being tweezed out one at a time. Then, the headaches start. First, the dull throb, pounding behind the eye sockets, the temples, the brain swelling like it's gonna crack right out of the cranium. The fluid builds in her pelvis and the lightness of nausea fills her stomach as she loses control of her bowels and feels the warmth of urine saturate the mattress below, and she's so relaxed and peaceful that she almost falls back asleep, but there's a knock-knock! And the door opens in one motion — Lemme guess. Ya sick again?! Well, listen ta me sweetie, your ass ain't goin' out all weekend if ya pullin' this shit again, I'll tell ya that. Coupla more absences and ya can say "bye-bye" to graduation. Not even halfway through the school year, and you've almost exceeded your absences! Shelly turns away and curls back into a ball. It ain't like that, ma. I'm really friggin' sick this time. I feel like I'm seriously gonna throw up. I think I have the — The flu? How many times ya have the flu this year, Shell? Huh? How many? Shelly moans and disappears back under the blanket. Look, I'm outta breath from this. I gotta leave. The new manager I hired last week didn't show up for the morning shift, so guess who has ta cover after doin' a 12-hour overnight? That's right, ya lookin' at'ah! And I *can't* call out sick! The door slams. Mom's gotta be a cunt about it like always. Tomorrow night the whole crews gonna be in the city at the Tunnel and Ima be stuck here drinkin' cups of tea, maybe poppin' a Xanax or two and watchin' a movie. Pfft. But she really is sick. And she really has used up all excuses possible to get out of all the things she didn't wanna do, especially gym class. Whatta drag. Who the fuck likes gym, anyway? Especially when ya gotta dope outfit on. Who wants ta change, put on your gym clothes, get sweaty, take them off, then put ya nice clothes back on? And she ain't usin' those nasty-ass showers either. So, screw it. If anytime she wasn't up for changin' and the gym teacher would yell out, "SHELLY O'CONNOR", she'd just say, "menstruating", and that meant...she ain't changin' a fuckin' thing....

2

———

THE TUNNEL, NYC

Jonathan knows it'll be a few hours before he settles down from waiting for the double-dipped acid to kick in and the dust blunt he shared with Mackey earlier when they got off the train really zoned him out and took an edge off the anticipation of the night (the pulsing strobes, the loud music, puke smeared bathroom, piss covered floors, the crowd stuffed into that shithole of a club where the walls look like they're folding in on ya when it darkens, then wondering why he was even goin' in the first fuckin' place). He sure as hell didn't dig bein' away from the action for so long, but he knows he can't wait on the couch that long, either. He carefully places the spiral pad on his lap and cuts a few lines of coke on it. Victor plops beside him and nudges his arm. Jonathan raises the pad to his nose and inhales one small, skinny line, then passes it to Victor, and he sniffs up a tiny bump, some of the white powder sticking to his mustache and goatee. Jonathan takes another few sniffs on a thick line, lights a cigarette, then sits back to listen to the music. After a few minutes, the music doesn't sound as fuzzy as it had, and the longer he listens to the DJ and gives the acid and coke more time, the better the music sounds. As a matter of fact, it isn't half bad. Who's he spinnin'? Victor leans into his ear, Aphex! This sonuvabitch is spinnin' Digeridoo! Jonathan shrugs, eh, it's good enough, though. I guess it's better than nothin', right? As if a shock of electricity hit him, Jonathan feels his chest and rubs it, the dull thud pulsing behind his breastbone. Mouth of cotton balls. Yo, I need some water. Victor leans in again, I gotchoo! No one's really got me, hahaha. Victor turns away and heads for the bar, and Jonathan tries to control the breaths in an effort to slow the heart and relax, but it ain't workin'. So, he tries to find a spot in the room to focus on to take his mind off the poundin' heart but instead finds a small curvaceous shape spinning before him with a stroboscopic effect. Long curly black hair whipping and a slivery shiny skirt moving up and down over her round brown thighs, coming toward him, rubbing herself all over, spinning, shaking to the music. Jonathan keeps his eyes low watching her legs, ankles, calves, knees, thighs, smiling smugly, wondering if the other ravers are looking at him wondering what he's looking at; if they are in fact seeing what he's seeing; if *he* is, in fact, seeing what he's seeing and not just part of the hallucinatory effects of a double-dipped tab of acid enhancing the experience. He grabs at a painful hard-on and tugs at it. The heart rate soars then slows down, only to speed back up again. The chest-flutters hit the throat with the bass of the music. He looks up to the laser light show bouncing off the walls and cutting through the dark shapes of the dancers, fascinated by the brightness thinking that they are a thousand spotlights and that he is the star. The slivery dress glitters in the brightness, cutting past his face with a trail of vanilla sugar under his nose, then her hair whips his eyes, her face to his face, It's all through my body, papi! This fuckin' ecstasy, the first time I took this shit; I've been dancin' for hours. I think it's almost morning! It's morning, right?! Grinding her jaw, gyrating her body. The sweat drips down her neck, into her cleavage. Beads of sweat shimmering on her thighs, dripping over her knees, and coming off the tip of her nose, onto her lips, her tongue curling up and licking it off— undulating around her mouth like a snake — her body still moving freely and smoothly, writhing, coiling. Jonathan reaches for her and misses as she twists away, but she notices this and turns back to him, and grabs for his hands placing them on each side of her hips, inching toward him until her pelvis is touching his nose and he breathes her in, opening his mouth but it's still filled with cotton. He glances at the bar to see what's up with Victor and the bottles of water and catches him talking up Lelah-Jean, his arm draped over her shoulder, massaging the area, his face brushing up against hers. But Jonathan sees somethin' different: Victor's mouth opening and his tongue licking her neck, turning to Jonathan curling his lips, sneering, taunting. That muthafucka, man, he's always gotta go for my exes, and I swear, I swear, he fucked Shelly down by the park last year; one of the first weeks we started seein' each other. And Jonathan jumps up and rushes the bar, shoving Victor away from Lelah-Jean, toppling over him, drinks cascading off the bar, liquor spilling, and Jonathan grabs his face, takes a piece of skin between his teeth, tears it from the jawbone. Victor squeals like a stuck pig. Jonathan mulls over the scene in his mind, looping over and over, watching the blood trickle down Victor's face, watching himself smashing the knuckles of his fists into Victor's skull, feeling the skin break apart under his nails and the bone beneath surfacing like a boil coming to a head. Jonathan grinds his jaw and shifts his focus back to the dancer, but his field of vision flickers into kaleidoscopes. The dancers, merely shapes of black, caught between the many colors of the strobe: the reds, the greens, the purples, and the bright, bright, BRIGHT WHITE blinding him with thousands of pulsations, throbbing, swelling, shrinking, then dispersing. Lelah-Jean slides next to him and quickly weaves her fingers through his. Gots ya water right here, sir. Jonathan grabs it without looking at her, takes a swig, and stuffs it in his backpack along with the spiral pad. She stares at his profile, sensing something is wrong, and waves her hand in front of his face, Yoooooo...everythin' good? Hello? Jonathan shoves her away and stammers to his feet, tellin' her to get the fuck away. Whaddya mean, get-the-fuck-away?! She grabs his arm and attempts to pull him toward her, but he pulls in the opposite direction and shouts, Whyn't ya go suck Victor's dick or somethin', okay? He pushes her away and then pushes himself through the dancers, and Lelah-Jean follows, yelling, grabbing at his arms, but the sweat-drenched skin makes him harder to hold than an eel. She manages to hook her nails into the back of his shirt while kicking at his heels. Get the fuck off me, bitch! He crashes into the wall nearest the unisex bathrooms and asks him to say that again, because she really didn't hear it. And he does. Nose to nose. Emphasizing the word *BITCH*. Saying it *in* her face, bits of saliva spraying off his lips onto her lips and in her eyes, and the anger and the hurt of anger enflame her chest and surges through the top of her shoulders and down her back and in one desperate flash she follows the icy impulse and smashes her knuckles against his forehead sending him spiraling to the ground. Kids pushing, swarming together, yelling, Break it up! Asking if he's okay. Jonathan gets to his feet, grabbing at her shirt, ripping the collar, pulling her in, and then shoving her back. The crowd moves as one peristaltic wave and carries Jonathan along its perimeter, his vision throbbing in and out of blackness. A red exit sign aglow. The white slants of light widen, guiding him, shaping a doorway opening, flickering among the abstractions. The dancers losing shape. Becoming the light around them. He steps through the shinning opening, now fully dilated, and finds himself cold in the early dawn of the bleak February. Lelah-Jean is in his face. There are tears. Cheeks red and enflamed. Her eyes are two frozen puddles reflecting the sky. She cries so hard she vomits on the sidewalk, splashing over his shoe. He wraps her tightly with a bear hug, squeezing, apologizing, but yelling, soundin' like a lost child screamin' for his mother. Always fuckin' wittem, always gotta be fuckin' wittem and touchin' 'im when I'm around so I see, and he's fuckin' with everyone, always; ya fuckin' hurt me over and over and do this to me so much and expect me not ta say shit about it. Lelah-Jean sobs on him, his fleece blotting the tears, and the scratches on her neck and face lightly trickle blood on her torn collar. The avenues are coming to life. Storefronts opening. Car engines roaring, Loud taxis screaming. New Yorkers swarm the sidewalks, increasing in number, folding Lelah-Jean and Jonathan into the backdrop of the living, moving, breathing city. Jonathan twists and jerks from his pain and tears. He opens his eyes almost wishing... hoping... but there is only blackness.

3

THE TOWN OF MY BIRTH

Her skin is raw and pink and littered with acne holes that look more like cigarette burns. But there's another liquid world below her that blows with the cold wind yet refuses to freeze. The puddle reflects the sky, and Shelly stares into it and spits. The ripples create a blur of the pines standing tall among the few passing clouds. Jonathan appears in the blur, his image wavering in the reflection. He spits into the puddle, too. I almost died a few nights ago, y'know. Shelly shrugs, I am so sad that you didn't. Jonathan shrugs, too. Whaddya wanna do today? It's fuckin' cold. She thinks about it for a few seconds, pushing the loose bleached white locks behind the white headband. I wanna visit the town of my birth. I wanna know my daddy's real last name. It's something Italian. It's not O'Connor? No. My mother kept her last name because they were never married. Duh! The only Mr. O'Connor is my fat ass grandfather. Yeah, ya know somethin'? He really does have a fat ass. He's like...pear-shaped. She looks back down to the puddle and regains her focus, staring deeply into their reflection. The sky clear and hard. The pine trees stand so tall it looks as if they touch the sky. Where is the town of your birth? South

Hampton. Fuck that! That's like two hours away. No, pussy, it's one hour, actually...by car...It's Wednesday. 11 am. There is no fuckin' traffic goin' out east. We can be there in forty-five minutes if you don't drive like a 90-year-old woman. She raises a candy ring pop to her mouth and sucks on it. She then passes her hand to Jonathan. He lowers his head and sucks on it too. When your lips are red like that, you look like a girl...like an ugly girl. Ha-ha-ha...fuck you. Oh! By-the-way. Not today, mon frère. I'm on the rag and it's heavy, heavy waterfall time for at least a week and maybe a few days. So; I don't mind? You're a gross-ass fuckin' pig. Jonathan lowers his head and sucks on her ring pop again. D'ya have an extra headwrap thing? My ears are cold. Yes. In my bag in your car. It's lavender, though. She looks him up and down. But it'll match what you're wearin'.

They both get in the car and drive off along Sunrise HWY. The sun slants through the pine barrens as they go eastward. Every so often, Jonathan glances over Shelly, who nods in and out of sleep. Her legs are long enough that her knees reach the dashboard while leaning back in the seat. The light hit her face, exaggerating the shining red acne bumps and uneven white skin mottled with dry, dark spots that could be concealer. He glances over at her and feels miserable. Feels like a total piece of shit for being around Lelah-Jean when Shelly wasn't there. For hurting Lelah-Jean so badly that she vomited all over his shoes. Since his sister died, he hasn't been the same. A part of him turned black. And he's worried the rest of him will go that way, too, and turn black. Like a cancer, each one of his organs will rot, stiffen, and burn up into ash. He pictures this happening. He watches himself driving the car and his entire body blowing away softly into a black dust cloud of burnt ash, dissolving from solids to air. He looks to her again. The song "Dagger" by Slowdive plays over in his mind. The line that goes, "The sunshine girl is sleeping." And he remembers swimming with her at Lake Ronkonkoma last summer, when she told him *I wanted ya ta look at me like the way I see ya lookin' at her; he dunked her head into the churning water like it was purified on the other end of the earth and came back a clean, clear liquid, and when she popped up, he told her he loved fucking her NOT LIKE A FRIEND, and she is everything to him.* He cracks a window and the cold air smells of pine. Shelly is asleep, face rested on her right shoulder and seatbelt, head bobbing along with the motion of the car. Sunrise HWY quickly bottles necks to one lane, as if time dissolved an hour into five minutes. This is the first time he has ever driven this far east. The desolate landscape makes him nervous. The ghastly pine barrens hang on the edges of the road like gaunt, raw, skeletons strung up along the HWY, reminding him of the dead soldiers he once saw back in high school on a WWII documentary. His palms ache and sweat as he grips the steering wheel, almost too scared to let go of it as if he might spin off the road and kill them both. There's' nothing more terrifying to him at this moment than being responsible for her death, being responsible for her removal from this earth is something he cannot bear. He rolls the window down further, hoping that cold pine air will keep him focused, soothe him, and Jonathan calms once more, allowing himself to be motionless behind the wheel, almost dead, as if he is absorbed by a dream, floating weightless on the fringes of some velvet cloud. Then, the light of the sun surrounds him, a light so complete and all-consuming that he experiences it in every part of his being, every ivory cell filling with the brightness of infinity. Then, slowly coming out of it as the first cloud covers the sun, his eyes flick up and close, and he knows it will be a good while before he ever experiences this feeling again. Jonathan wakes her up, and she guides him the rest of the way to the Town Hall, where they find a shaded parking spot furthest away from the weathered white building. Jonathan goes to the trunk and opens it. Shelly is right beside him and asks him, How many bodies ya back there this time? He looks at her and tells her to fuck off and grabs a bubble jacket and puts it on before closing the trunk. Shelly hooks her arm through his arm and tells him, We look like hobos. Jonathan's brow sinks to a "V" as his hands feel around inside the jacket pockets. Two cherry bombs? How the fuck did they get in here? Maybe from last summer with his aunt when they'd go into Chinatown to get fireworks for the 4th, but why are they inna winter jacket? Jonathan fumbles with them inside the pocket, rolling them between his fingers, then in his palms until they get inside the Town Hall. And they can tell immediately the village clerk is such a bitch with that cat-like squint. She can't be bothered with them. There's no one inside the joint and she'd love for it to stay that way. One look at these two sauntering in, she knows they're from "up island", almost identically dressed in awful, second-hand Salvation Army clothing, threaded and warn. Their jeans are way too big, and the frayed, dirty, blackened ends drag on the floor. The oversized layers of clothes hang from their jackets. They may look like a coupla ragdolls but the multiple colors somehow accentuate the appearance falling nearly perfectly and artfully into each garment with natural grace. The lavender headband that covers Jonathan's ears goes with the green shirt peeking out beneath the black bubble jacket, and Shelly's reds and yellows are offset by the white-white headband and bleached-out hair with fading pink tips washed lightly and unevenly throughout the strands. Her diamond-studded labret piercing just below the thickness of her bottom lip glitters off the bright light slicing in from the windows slants behind the old salty clerk. Hi. This is the town of my birth, and I would like a copy of my birth certificate. The clerk spits out a piercing snarl. Okay, but I will need your identification first, young man. Jonathan spits out a piercing snarl back at the clerk and tells her she's a girl as Shelly hands over her Junior License, pointing to her name: MICHELLE ANN O'CONNOR. The clerk snaps it away and disappears into the back filing room. She emerges moments later with a giant white binder filled with birth certificates encased in plastic. O, O, O, O, O-C, O'CONNOR... here we go. Michelle? Michelle *Ann* O'Connor? Yes, she answers in a dropped tone. A whisper. Her eyes divert from the clerks' eyes. Something is troubling her from within. Vulnerability showing, but keeping her thoughts and emotions inward. She touches the plastic that covers her birth certificate, her little finger tracing the letters of his very long last name. That's $20 for the copy and a $5 processing fee. Twenty-five bucks! I don't have twenty-five dollars! Jonathan steps up, hunches his shoulders, and tilts his head, extending a hand with a Mastercard. I do, he tells the clerk. The clerk eyes him disdainfully and her crimped half-crooked sneer lets him know she doesn't trust him either, but takes the card anyway. I need your I.D., too. Yeah, I got it here. Hold up. And he hands her over his license. The clerk sighs and checks over the license while Jonathan becomes distracted and consumed by a large black and white picture behind framed glass resting against the wall next to the entrance. Shelly is consumed by her father's name at the bottom of the birth certificate. She traces the outline of the letters of his name with her pointer finger, moving her lips soundlessly, *he writes just like me; it looks just like my signature*

Uh, young man.... can you not touch that, please? Jonathan turns around, crinkling his brow, and asks why and she tells him, it's a picture of value. That picture says nothing. A bunch of people standin' inna flood, lookin' confused. The fuck is so special 'bout it? It's historic and cannot be replaced. So, please do not touch it — thank you! Jonathan rolls the cherry bombs around in his pocket, eyes narrowing, face tightening and slightly wincing, removing the bombs, twisting the fuses together, eyeing Shelly, telepathically telling her it's time to leave, and with birth certificate in hand, she does, but her exit is cool and graceful and shrugs off the scene without a care. Jonathan lights the double fuse and tosses the bombs at the gibbering clerk. The explosion is sharp and cracks through the dry cold air like a clap of thunder. He then reaches inside his jacket for a can of lighter fluid and douses the entire area, especially the picture, saturating it until there is no more fluid. He lights a pack of matches, tosses the wavering flame to the floor, and exits. As they walk toward the parking lot, they both turn and watch the Town Hall blazing up all the way to the heavens, becoming one with the sun. Each smiling inwardly thinking about the end of their problems and the panic, at least for them. At least for now—

--Young man, did'ya hear me?! Jonathan stares at her while Shelly tells the clerk that his name is Jonathan as it says right there on his license. Yeah, can ya just run my credit card and give her a copy of her birth certificate so we can get the fuck outta here, please? The clerk snarls, exposing her front teeth. Jonathan approaches Shelly and says aloud, but not loud enough for the clerk to hear, that her teeth are so yellow he can't believe it's not butter. Shelly laughs, though she doesn't find it funny, and pinches his side. The clerk and her ugly snarl return with the copy of Shelly's birth certificate, so they can finally leave that place, and not exactly how Jonathan dreamed it, with the entire Town Hall, clerk included, burning up in a blazing pyre, but exiting as two teens would, awkwardly and a bit confused and aloof. Something was off about him, though, and Shelly felt it. It looks as if he's sleepwalking through the parking lot right into the driver's seat and hauling down the road, not even looking where he is going (turning left on red and coming to a complete stop at yellow). He is thinking, I should not have stopped prayin' when I was a kid. Then he no longer hears the horns honking. He no longer hears the Shelly's voice. He hears now only the myriad and everlasting cicadas, leaning in the window, breathing the hot still lush fragrance of the earth, thinking of how when he was a kid, he had loved darkness, of walking or sitting alone among trees at night, looking up at them as if they were ancient gods. Then the ground, the bark of trees, became actual, savage, filled with, evocative of, strange and baleful half delights and half terrors. He was afraid of it. He feared; he loved being afraid and especially being afraid with Maggie by his side. Listening to the frogs at night, by the lake, chirping back and forth to one another and the trees breathing and swelling around them, protecting them from the unknown that lies beyond their darkness. Then one day, while lounging in the backyard, he realized he was no longer afraid of darkness. He just hated it; he would flee from it to walls, to artificial light. Yes, he thinks. I should never have stopped praying. I should never have given my only rosary beads to Marielle. She took them to the earth with her! He turns from the coldness of the car window and rolls it up, but the images from the memories consume him and the street beyond the window becomes one wall of the study which is lined with books. He pauses before them, seeking, until he finds the one which he wants. It is Blake. It is the portable Blake — a book he stole from the Seaville library his senior year. He has had it ever since. He sits beneath the natural light from a window and opens it. It does not take long. Soon, the fine galloping language, the gutless swooning full of sapless tress, and dehydrated lusts begin to swim smooth and swift and peaceful. It is better than praying without having to bother to think aloud. It is like listening in a cathedral to a eunuch chanting in a language that he does not even need to not understand, and it is Shelly's voice that commands him where to turn, mixing with sounds of traffic and his memories blending, blending, bleeding in and out of a reality which stings him malevolently like the whipping wind of cruel February. Where are you? Where are you, right now? Jonathan shakes his head, the words not coming, only the gesticulation. Tell me where you are in your mind, Jonathan. He quickly responds, I miss her. I want her back here with me on earth, alive, breathing, and really alive. I should've never stopped prayin'. She'd still be alive. I'd still be... I feel like... I am lost. Jonathan's right hand falls off the wheel and onto the center console. Shelly brushes her palm across his knuckles and tells him, But you're here with me right now and at least we have each other. Her lithe, pretty fingers lace with his. Her eyes swell, reddening with tears dripping down to her lips. Turn up here. There's a private beach my mom use ta take me that I want ya to see. He turns to Shelly and sees Maggie: a wavering flickering image of light slanting through the passenger window and glowing gleefully, swelling with radiance before dissolving back to Shelly.

They park along the dead-end street surrounded by a harbor, lapping over the soggy beach grass, the color of wheat. Shelly leads him through a sandy path and over a dune to the private beach. The wind is strong and cold so they keep their faces down, hiding in the creases of their arms, shielding the stinging sand from their skin. Neither of them knows how long they'll last, but this place means a lot to Shelly, and she hasn't been here since the 80s when she was a kid. We'll hafta come back here this summer, but those words don't sit right in her stomach, as if she half means it. The lightness of fear fills her belly as if she senses something tragic about making plans, any plans for her future, especially with Jonathan. Her skin vibrates beneath the soft cotton clothes, but of the cold currents, of the blackness of a fear deeply embedded in her bones that speaks to her, and of her, shooting the impulse to the brain to interpret the feeling as death. And she begins to see lady death everywhere her eyes blink: the sea, the waves, on the foam of the waves, the sky, hanging on the clouds, going black, the driftwood, the empty shells, the seaweed, the sand, and in the dark liquid pupils and hazy swells of the fading brightness of Jonathan's sun-bleached aura. Anything to distract this feeling and reduce the fidget coldness, she jumps and yawps like a tortured banshee, We should fight then to keep warm! She latches to his back like a chicken fight, biting his ear, messing his hair, raking it with her nails. His knees give and they fall to the sand. She straddles him and pins his arms down. I can spit right in ya face and ya can't do shit about it. A calm, impassive look crosses his face as his lips open and she lowers her face over his and dribbles a long strand of saliva onto his slow unfolding tongue. She kisses him deeply, their tongues moving around, swirling fluids back and forth, feeding a connected movement with earth, sea, wind, the clear, hard sky, and even the sand whipping up and stinging their skin — they are heavenly entwined and as the emotions increase, Jonathan ruins it all by swatting her away and accidentally hitting across her chest. Ow! Oh-my-fuckin-God! You hit my tit, you cocksucker! You know how sore they are this time of month? Jonathan turns on his side and pulls the collar over his chapped ears, rising to his feet and finally removing the cherry bombs from his pocket. These are illegal. *Really* illegal. I got 'em in the Chinatown with my aunt and Maggie, last summer. She knew this little place at the bottom of this whack-ass laundromat and they sold all these super rare and super dangerous fireworks. He had a whole bag of these muthafuckas and I lit most of 'em off that fourth of July, but I somehow have two left and I have no idea how they got in this jacket, and it's really buggin' me out. Jonathan stares at them, thinking, thinking, remembers finally loving the darkness of that moment, of that night lit with the beauty of electric colors exploding and fizzling across the sky, of Maggie jumping gleefully as the Mortars burst into the air. A purple glow. He turns from Maggie as she fades with embers of last 4th of July, and faces Shelly. I wanna light these muthafuckas off right now and throw them to the sea but it's too fuckin' windy, y'know? They'll never light. All I gots is matches. Shelly looks to the sky and thinks: I gotta a zippo in my bag but...yeah, that probably won't light either cos of this stupid wind. Ya can still throw them to the sea, though. It could be ceremonial. You don't need the explosion. Jonathan studies the cherry bombs as they roll together in the palm of his right hand. Nah, I'm gonna hold on to 'em. Y'know, I got somethin' in the trunk I shouldn't have...and I think maybe I should get ridda that, too. Shelly steps closer to him. Her headband falling over her eyes: What is it? Jonathan takes her back to the car, opens the trunk and they both gaze into the blackness. He pulls up the underboard and beneath it lies a spare tire, and a sawed-off shotgun by its side. A plastic Ziplock bag is attached to the trigger. Inside are four red shotgun shells. Shelly's eyes shiver. Her face whitens and holds within it the darkness of fear. WHY THE FUCK DO YOU STILL HAVE THAT, her voice stammering and shaking an unsteady and uneven pitch, softer and an octave higher than her usual voice. He looks at her but doesn't say a word. He grabs the gun and bag of shotgun shells, slams the trunk closed, and marches back toward the beach. Listen shit-for-brains! If ya fire that thing off someone's gonna hear it from one of those rich-ass bungalows and call the cops and we're fucked! Jonathan continues marching on, the back of his black shinning coat shimmering in the bleached sunlight. Shelly screams after him: Ya remember bein' in court? Remember what that was like?! Huh?! Y'all got off easy! Easy! Makin' things *hard* again, Jacky boy! Nothin' fuckin' new here! Jonathan shouts to the wind and it dulls his words and cripples his flesh with angst. Shelly shouts after him, and her words go silent in the wind. She pitches her voice higher, What ya say?! He raises his arms, saying, CERIMONIAL! It's supposed ta be cer-i-mon-ial! RIGHT?! She catches up and stands before him. The ocean waves clap the shoreline, just nipping the worn-out rubber heels of his airwalks. He remembers opening the bedroom door and there was a weight behind it, clunking, a dull thud, on the other side, and Nickelodeon was on her TV and turning the knob, and opening the door, and the sun bleeding in from the aluminum blinds. His sisters body, small, twisted, wretched, hanging by the crystal knob, bending but not breaking from the door. Her neck, like rubber, dangling from her shoulders, blood and saliva dripping in warm pools, her face swollen green and yellow, and her eyes inflated like two balloons. He cut her down and held her in his arms. The sunlight bleeds through the blinds filling the room with bleached-brightness. Shelly hugs him and her warmth brings him back to the beach and the sea. To his ear, she whispers, she's still here inside you; like me. Pretty soon, they'll be warmth, love, suntan lotion, laughter, towels, and naps in the sun. Jonathan remembers being back in Maggie's room where his parents scream at him while he holds her, WHAT HAPPENED?! As he watches her lithe image near the window wave goodbye and dissolve into the yellow slants of sunlight, he pulls away from Shelly and fires a few rounds into the sea, thinking, I should have never done it in the first place. I should've never fired this fuckin' thing outta the Monte Carlo. Why'd I do it? Why'd they do it? Why'd they bring me there to do it? The buckshot's killed a dog. Hit a baby's shoulder. But it did not die. Blew out a tire on a firebird. Broke a front porch window. It was meant to blow apart a mailbox. I should've been prayin' instead Just like when the group home boys raped her Beat her and she was so ashamed she choked herself to death with a shoelace and hooked it around her bedroom doorknob My Maggie My little sister Sweet child I shoulda been prayin' with you instead God did not stop you from doin' it but I coulda and I went after them with the sawed-off's and got one in the leg and one in the back and it ripped right through him blew the flesh off the bone and he died right there but not one of the group home boys ratted me out 'cos One life for one life EVEN STEVEN But she didn't hafta die and neither did he My sister My heart My blood A tear falls down his face, but he doesn't even feel it. Shelly kisses the wetness and hugs him hard, pressing her chapped lips to his ear: Take that ugly gun...all the death inside it and throw it to the sea. Her words are slower than her mouth. There's too much evil in that metal and wood. Jonathan breaks away and looks to the waves, breathing in the coldness and breathing out the blackness. Then, dashing toward the biggest wave, he hurls the gun into the air, envisioning a great white shark shooting out of the ocean and swallowing it up with one bite.

The sawed-off falls into a rolling swell and disappears in rings of white foam. Shelly has him in a bear hug, repeating that all of it is gone over and over until he tells her, I wanna be with it. Gone forever. Swallowed up into the void. Her lips move slower than the words when she says, Then I'll follow you. I'll follow you into forever —

And they dissolve into the bleached slants of yellow sun slicing the tops of the ocean waves.

4

———

TAPE 1: SIDE A

Mackey cranks the music on his car radio and yells over it: This is Ninja Tune's latest. Zen Brakes, Volume One! Only available on vinyl. When I transferred it to tape, I didn't even use the EQ. Listen to this shit. The sound is so fuckin' deep and warm. Listen to these lows. They just hum! Lelah-Jean kicks the driver's seat and tells him to lower the fuckin' music. Kick my seat again, bitch, and watch what happens! Say that ta me when you're not drivin' and watch where my foot ends up, muthafucka. Everyone in the car gins broadly as possible and chuckles, their heads bouncing and bobbing like they're used to this bantering bullshit. Shelly giggles and takes drags on her cigarette, bouncing on Jonathan's lap, passing the butt to his lips so he can have a pull. The smoke is so thick and opaque in the car that everyone's movements seem stroboscopic. Chris hunches over in the passenger seat rolling a blunt. This time around the boys had the good shit: special k, angel dust, and Brooklyn Bombs (that's ecstasy mixed with heroin). Take it together, and ya can either reach the legends of the highest heavens or get totally fucked, and end up reelin' in a fiery hell, with your world spinnin' in webs of vertigo for days on end. You'll wish you were dead just to stop the misery. But the worst part is, you live another day. And another one after that. Spinnin' in a vertigo world, and it won't consume you totally, like anything that is representative of a place of damnation and eternal torment, you will continue within the spin cycle half alive...or half dead. Whichever way you choose to look at it. You'll have moments that'll seem clear and less nauseous and ambiguous, only for the whole acid ride to begin again. And again. And again, until it finally, but ever so gradually stops. Why do this in the first place? No other explanation than boredom. There is *absolutely* no other reason why. Same reason why the crew decided, at 12:am on a Monday night, that taking a trip to the north shore and visiting some teenage witch's grave that died sometime in the early 19th century was the "cool thing to do". Mary's Grave, as everyone calls it. And it's not really a grave; it's actually an ancient stone playhouse on a cliff overlooking the Harbor. Apparently, she was hanged there when the townspeople found her sleeping next to her father's corpse, which was all hacked up and rotting. It was dawn, and the stench of death was palpable. Ya could smell it from a mile away — ENOUGH OF THIS STUPID FUCKIN' STORY! Shelly pinches Jonathan's side, then cups her hands over her ears. I've heard it so many times that I'm gonna bleed out my ears. She killed her father and some animals in her playhouse, and the village folk hung her 'cos they thought she was a witch. Shelly takes her hands from her ears and folds them across her tummy. Mackey tells Jonathan to keep going anyway because he ain't ever heard the whole story. There is no "whole story". Jonathan made most of it up. Bullshit, I did! Yeah, yeah, you're always makin' shit up. Chris turns around from the passenger seat. Yeah, he's always lyin', but this story's been around for a long-ass time, man. I remember hearin' about it from one of my dad's friends a while back, and I heard if someone pisses in her playhouse your car engine stops, and someone dies—

4. Tape 1: Side B

CHRIS WAS thirteen the first time he was arrested. And it happened at a cemetery. Halloween of '89, he was hangin' with the Group Home boys and got caught tryin' to steal the dead bodies of the inmates that one-time belonged to the old, abandoned Kings Point Psychiatric Asylum. As the story goes, Chris dug a few feet down, and the earth swallowed him right up. Both feet touching the top of the coffin. Feeling the old wood bend like rubber, slowly givin' way as the heaviness of the soil and Chris' body pushed into skull and bone. And that's how the cops found him. Waist deep in the earth dressed in some scrubby homemade Halloween costume: a dirty sheet and a green plastic witch mask. But the cops who caught them wanted to make an example of them for the rest of the kids in the neighborhood, despite the fact that they were minors. They were arrested, booked, and brought before a judge in their Halloween costumes, who found it difficult to retain his laughter as he made Chris promise to be a good boy and not deface public property or next time the punishment would be severe. *Young man, this is a Class H felony, without authorization of law or the consent of the surviving spouse or next of kin of the deceased, to knowingly and willfully disturb, destroy, remove, vandalize, or desecrate any human remains that have been interred in a cemetery. The penalty for this crime is typically one term of imprisonment not to exceed one year and/or a fine of up to $10,000. Do you understand this, son? Do you understand the next I find you in my courtroom for the aforementioned crime, I will throw your little ass in jail without hesitation. Nod if you understand this.*

A few weeks later he stole a car. This time it was with Mackey, who's a year older. They'd walk the streets around 3 or 4 am. Mackey's dad was a locksmith, and he carried his old man's Sim Jim and worked it like a pro. They'd hit low-end cars, nothing that brought them too much attention. Busted Cavaliers, Toyotas, Datsun's, station wagons, and they'd drive them all around, pick up their friends for school, get high, and when the cars ran out of gas, they'd leave it where they were. One of the cars had a 9mm in the glove compartment. Mackey was like, Muthafucka! And bullets! Full metal fuckin' jacket. He secreted it all in his backpack. The dumbass wound up settin' it off in the boy's room when he plopped it on the floor to take a piss. It blew a hole right through the bathroom stall door, missing Chris's big blonde head by a few inches. He shot up off the bowl and lurched face forward, pants around the ankles. They were each caught, but Chris was released. Mackey was the one that was placed in a youth detention center for two years. They were caught many times stealing cars, but Chris was always released after promising not to do it again. He was so young, with that big round stupid head and that moppy blonde Dutch-boy haircut, looking so young and innocent-looking that it was impossible for a judge to think of him as a criminal, and they were hesitant about sending him to the institutions where he might learn to be a professional criminal rather than just a mischievous hood. But not Mackey. Man, he got the brunt of everything, and they sent his ass straight to juvie. When he was released, he looked like a grown man at only seventeen. Mackey was bigger and stronger than most kids his age and took great pride in his ability to fight. He showed Chris and Jonathan a stick-and-poke tattoo of an anarchy symbol he got in the ditch of his arm while serving time. Soon enough, he moved on from pot to cocaine and ecstasy. Upon returning from juvie, Mackey's mother noticed him burning his arm with cigarettes and writing on his books and bedroom walls "Fuck my life" and "My life sucks." Mackey started crushing up his dad's MS Contin pills and snorting them. One morning he took a whole bottle of his mother's Xanax, vomiting most of it before it could kill him. Weeks later, he wrote a note saying he was "going where the sea meets the sky" before disappearing overnight. Police helicopters found him in a daze at Seaville Beach, where he put up a fight and was cuffed and taken in a straitjacket to a psychiatric hospital. But Mackey was crafty, his mother would say. He didn't let the psychiatrist know that he had left a death note, that he was going to kill himself, and then the doctor released him. In April, he and Chris were caught in his house, wired on coke and gathering his mother's jewelry to pawn for more drugs. His mother brought him to rehab and then to a psychiatrist. Again, he dodged treatment. His mother said, Every time we'd bring him somewhere, he seemed to be able to sweet-talk his way out of it and then he'd come home and be good for a day and then start again. He'd tell Chris stories about juvie and how he used to sneak away to smoke angel dust and sniff horse tranquilizer; now all he wants to do is skateboard and get his GED. There was something about spending time in the detention hall that he enjoyed. He'd go down to the pizzeria, where all the boys hung out, playing video games and buying endless rounds of cokes, garlic knots, and slices, sitting there in wrap-around booths, telling stories about the shit he's seen "doing time." None of the kids could relate. They weren't from the nicest areas, but, still, none of 'em took their antics to the places Chris and Mackey did. He told them about two boys who blew a kid's head off while they were diving down the Belt Parkway. It was a part of a gang initiation. He bragged about knowing both of them while "locked up." Ol' Jonathan, or "Jacky-boy" as they'd sometimes call 'em just to get 'im all pissy, was so influenced by Mackey's stories and his transformation that he got his own version of the

anarchy tattoo, but on the palm side of his right wrist. Chris'
parents were a whole different story. His mother abandoned
them before his twelfth birthday and is living with his dad's
brother somewhere in the Keys. But no one really knows. His
father, this big-ass grizzly bear of a man, hates him and would
beat the shit outta him, even right in front of his friends. One
day while they were hunting, Chis wound cursing out his old
man and got the butt of a bolt action rifle to the eye. Twenty-two
stitches and six hours of plastic surgery later, he still got that
bright slug-shaped scar cutting his left eye in half. The incident
nearly blinded him, but no one ever heard him say a word
about it —

4. Tape 2: Side A

Chris slaps his palms on the dashboard, Yo, it's down this
road over here; where the fuck ya goin'? No, it's not! That'll take
us back around the loop again, ya bozo. Jonathan leans forward,
waving his hands, No, no, no, no! It's right over here — down off
Mt. Misery Road. Make a right make a right make a right, right
here quick. Mackey pushes closer to the steering wheel, flashing
the high beams, I know where the fuck I am. The car wobbles as
it slowly spirals down a dark road like a funhouse roller coaster.
They share hits of ecstasy and Special K, and Chris breaks open
a bottle of Old E. Jonathan swallows a tab of acid and extends
his neck out the passenger side window, looks up at the sky, and
sees there are no stars. The sky is a blank slate hidden behind a
thick grey gauze, slowly parting. Mackey slides a tape into the
tape deck, and industrial sounds hit the air. Each kid rocking
their head, passing around the old E, as the others slap their legs
or the back of the seats and dashboard; squealing and pointing
at the canopy trees as the car finds Grimms Bay on Harbor Road
just off Mt. Misery — that beautiful Bay partially frozen crys-

talline immaculate under the light of the moon. The old stone playhouse of Mary rests under husks of dead beach grass and spidery arms of dead vines. Jonathan steps out and sees vibrant, rich Mandalas overhead extending down with Shiva and the many arms and the dark Spanish face of Mariella; innocent, bronze, glimmering then melting to a gibbering ghastly and ghostlike clown. Lelah-Jean falls over Shelly and Mackey trips, spilling the bottle of Old E on the grass as Chris lurches forward to catch it, but the bottle never falls, and Chris only swats the pebbles and debris off the road. Lelah-Jean swipes the bottle from Mackey, and he goes back to the car for his knapsack and takes out a small Super 8 video camera and flashlight, whirling around filming everything and everyone that passes by his field of vision. Jonathan grabs Shelly from behind and bites down on her clavicle, saying, You're like an angel bleeding eternity's red river of soulless bodies. But she hates when he talks like this, so she pushes him away, smelling winter off his clothes — a crisp scent of pine and apple.

INSIDE THE PLAYHOUSE

Chris places a featureless mask over his face, telling Mackey, I AM THE SHAPE, while a tightly rolled blunt is lit. Placed. Through. The. Mouth hole. Of the mask and Mackey filming it all. The flashlight bounces, the shadows dancing/leaping, the arms of the dead vines wavering in the light, and the trees, the leafless trees swaying, as Chris takes the angel-dust of the formaldehydes deep into the tiny sacks of his lungs and it's like menthol to him. Wintery, earthy menthol beauty as Chris exhales in mindfulness, grounding himself, looking as calm as a monk in a picture. Mackey finds a corner and pees all over the wall.

BACK ON THE STREET

Lelah-Jean folds in and hugs herself, feeling the effects-tasy burning through her veins and tickling her skin with invisible feathers. She rocks back and forth on the sand, the icy waves burping and fizzling over the frozen earth, her eyes skyward finding the stars glinting in and out of the grey ghostly strands. Jonathan and Shelly are tangled together, going round and round near the playhouse, spinning closer to the bluff. And Jonathan, he watches the frosted top of the harbor unfreeze and move in boundless colors of greens, blues, and gold, and Shelly watches the shadows become monsters and the flashlight from the playhouse and the arms of the canopy trees are bare and they look like claws —

Descending

Down

Upon

Them.

And it's as if Shelly suddenly says to her mouth, We're fuckin' doomed. Jonathan laughs, falling backward over the dead beach grass. Look, Shelly says pointing up, They're comin' for us. She hears the branches rattling in the wind like a string of paper dolls, the skeletal hands and fingers between the deafening whistling breeze Lelah-Jean comes up blazing, her face sloped down into Jonathan's pursed blowing mouth as Shelly stands there, eyes flickering heavenward. Thin. Bright. Darkness. Jonathan turns away from Lelah-Jean, pushing her down, Ya can't do that right now. Ya just can't, so fuck off. Lelah-Jean grabs the earth with both hands, pouts, and grinds her jaw. You know for sho, don't ya? Well, I'll do what I want. Shelly, her back to them, faces the harbor, hypnotized by the stars and the trees. From here one could just see the roof trees of the playhouse, frosted in moonlight.

INSIDE THE PLAYHOUSE

Ya hear that? The woods are alive, man. Mackey moves the camera closer to Chris. A childlike fright looms in his widening pupils, gagging on a mouthful of smoke. I fuckin' hear nothin', yo. But I tell you this. I can't feel my lips. I can't feel my tongue, either. The vines and the shadows extending from the wall dance along the wind currents between the camera and the light. The smoke becoming so thick and blue that it makes the room look as if a small part of the light blue sky has somehow fallen into the room. Mackey points the camera at Chris again. The flashlight dims. Chris, now an inert lump, half black against the stones, dangles a hand off the side of the bench. Mackey stops filming. There is something he hears. A breath, warm, close to his ear. The dark odor. A feline scent. A thin whisper. The branches clatter as the wind passes over them, blowing like a cat growls. The flashlight cuts a flicker and then goes black.

AT THE BLUFF, JUST BEFORE THE HARBOR

Lelah-Jean sings to herself a soft song, digging her heels into the grass and pushing her body up the side of the bluff. The coldness stings her lips. There is something around her she can feel but cannot see, and the wind growls like a cat.

SHELLY & JONATHAN

Sit Indian-style across from one another, about a yard away from Lelah-Jean. Shelly examines his face. An impassive stare. All of it, and yet nothing, looking right back at her. A shiver fills her stomach. Jonathan moves closer to her face, tugs at the zipper that goes around her neck like a track, and asks, Wouldya ever kill yaself? NOPE. She doesn't even think about it and silences him with a kiss over the mouth. She cries to herself, knowing he was probably thinking of Maggie. She then pulls away from his face and tells him, Ya should wear your glasses, y'know that. I love 'em in you. On you. Ya should wear them more often. Ya really should. Lelah-Jean moves in the blackness and Shelly becomes aware of her movement; something about her changes, and she whispers, The world is filled with people who tell ya what ya wanna hear, and the second ya turn your back ya hear what they really hafta say. Her mind flashes to a few moments ago when she was looking at the sky lost in her thoughts yet knowing Lelah-Jean was talkin' some shit to Jonathan, that she really couldn't hear, but gave her the vibe something wasn't right. Something was off about what she was saying to him.

MARY'S GRAVE, the end.
   The ghost of confusion gallops swiftly through the soul.

4. Tape 2: Side B

LELAH-JEAN DRIFTS to Jonathan and Shelly as if she's sleepwalking. Her words slur off her tongue with a feathery lightness, Hey, let's try talkin' ta Mary. Let's do a séance or somethin'. Communicate with her or some shit. Shelly stands up and attempts to answer, but her throat constricts, and tears rapidly build up behind her eyes. She keeps blinking them back and suddenly notices herself dressed in her former sweet sixteen gown, her hair a beautiful bleached white, sauntering across the sand, so svelte, so sexy. The dress, whispering while she moves. There is something she hears. A breath. An animal moans, soft and shuddering. A crackling footstep across the frozen ground. The high, sweet, evil laugh of a child —
   I am afraid.
   A blackness of a semi-solid form faces her and she can smell it and the wind comes off the Harbor, chilling her to the bone. She falls to a dense shadow of frozen shrubbery, hearing the wind blow and then die away.
   I am afraid.
   The spot suddenly looks familiar to her, one that brings her back two years ago to a bloody Halloween fight. But that was

another time, another life. Now everything is still, quiet, the earth coolly suspiring. The dark fills with voices, both familiar and unfamiliar, then faces circling around her. Jonathan, Lelah-Jean, Mackey, and Chris – their faces and voices, myriad, out of all time she had known, as though all the past was a dreary pattern. And going on through tomorrow night, all the tomorrows, to be a part of the dreary pattern, going on and on and on. She thinks of that with quiet astonishment: going on, myriad, familiar, since all that had ever been was the same as all that was to be since tomorrow to-be and had-been would be the same. Then, it was time. She rose.

I am so scared.

She drifts from the shadowy spot, floating around the car and entering the backseat. The car is dark. She peers out the window and floods of childhood return before her eyes. *I want the sun chasing me again; keep goin', faster, Ma. The woods are blockin'! Go faster so I can see it again! It's a dream...it looks just. Like. A. dream...The sky misty, sun bleeding through a summer dusk in June.* Y'all livin' in a fuckin' movie! Hear me?! Stupid, dramatic assholes! She's gonna be fine! She's gonna be alright! Mackey screams and goes on and on. Jonathan and Lelah-Jean hold Shelly in the backseat as her body thrashes and shakes. Her face contorting. Foam spitting from the mouth and undulating tongue. The whites of their eyes beaming, watching this, and Chris sitting shotgun, mesmerized by everything. Mackey turns the key and hits the gas, but the engine won't turn over. The headlights dim and then go black. There's no life. C'mon, ya ol' bitch, don't lemme down now. C'mon, ya can do it, fucker. Mackey tries again, again, hitting the gas and turnin' the key. Chris laughs and mutters to himself, It's like they said, ya pee in the playhouse and the car goes dead, just like they said. And the headlights flick on, the high beams lighting the dark road, then go dim, then flash on high.

And there are prayers
& yelling
& screeching
SHELLY, DON'T DIE — PLEASE
SHE'S NOT BREATHIN'!
They are crowding the backseat, squishing together
YES, SHE IS! LOOK! HER CHEST IS MOVIN'!
Jonathan prays aloud in a dry, suffocated voice,
HOLY MARY MOTHER OF GOD
HOLY MARY MOTHER OF GOD
HOLY MARY MOTHER OF GOD
PRAY FOR US SINNERS NOW AND AT THE HOUR OF OUR DEATH, AMEN.

Mackey banging on the steering wheel, PLEASE START. PLEASE, GOD. I DON'T NEED THIS GIRL DYIN' ON ME, and the car bucks and shakes and the headlights flicker on the dark road, then go dim, and then flash again to a large, white dog. The dog backs away, barking, foaming, howling. Chris extends his left leg over the console and presses his foot over Mackey's foot, yelling for him to GO. A long, whiskered face of snow comes at them like a hovering specter, appearing in the driver's side mirror, echoing back, GO! The car engine finally turns over, and Mackey puts it in drive and shoots down the road. His eyes not focusing. All the kids hollering at once, waving their hands around, giving instructions on where to turn. But Mackey, man, he just keeps driving and driving. Those beady eyes of his spread far apart on his face like a mole, trying to focus on where the hell he's going. Swears he just passed over the same bridge twice and thinking they were heading right back to where they were stuck the first time. But there was a turn right over there where it forks off, and the General Store is smack dead on the corner. Jonathan swears to God that's the way to go and to bare left, TRUST HIM. So he does, and finally there are some lights...

some streetlights, and soon after it was the town, then Middle Road, then Nichols Road for another five miles south, then main street...then Seaville. Then, home. No need for the hospital tonight. Shelly is coming to, head on Jonathan's lap, bouncing away, eyes regaining sight. Hearts slowing to sinus rhythm. No talking. Just the engine going loud over Ninja Tunes rattling those car speakers like a rock in a tin can. And the rattling lulls everyone down to a nice, soft rest on a winter's night. Coulda made a baby go beddy-bye.

5

THE GHOST IS STILL WITH US

Shelly, in the fetal position holding the TV remote, switching between MTV and Charlie's Angels reruns, looks literally dead. Zombified. This horrible seasick feeling swirls in her gut, gnawing away at it like a little rat. If she gets up too fast, the burning sensation in her stomach will increase the queasiness and force her to throw up. There's the Mylanta, right there next to her television, but any sudden movement may set off the eruption of vomit. The watery mouth. The throat contractions. The bitter bile hitting the back throat, and for the next several hours it will continue. So, if she stays perfectly still watching the Real-World reruns, she might fall asleep and wake up feeling less nauseous. She traces her hand along the stitching of her favorite pink, velvety pillow she sewed herself last year. Her mother walks in without knocking and places a mug of tea on the end table next to her bed. Her eyes are like two dark crevasses in a rock. She's already in the middle of a story about work drama about the Group Home she manages and how the goddamn overnight staff always gotta call out last minute leaving it to her to cover the shift. I can neva get anyone last minute ta cova these fuckin' overnights! And that stupid on-call list is for shit! No one eva picks up tha phone! Okay, I'm off to Hell again. Feel betta. Ya know the numba if ya need anything. *Mom's life is a rerun. A never-ending loop of the same old shit every week.* Shelly's eyes never leave the television screen. The wide icy glow of her irises and the soft rings of gold around them. The sun barely penetrates the blackout curtains. The blue glow of the television. A commercial for the new music videos airing tonight on 120 Minutes flashes over. Gene Loves Jezebel comes on just as her eyes flicker and then close one final time. She hears the song evaporating into her unconscious mind. "Your beauty has spoken, with eyes that shine... my resistance crumbles, I stumble, I fall...". *Her mother strokes her forehead, and the doctors stick a tube down her throat and tell her to stay still. Her body squirms, and her legs kick. The IV bag falls over and hits the ground. It crashes to the ground! Mom! Mother! Ma! Help me! Give me something. Please. Anything! I need to be calm! Try and relax, Michelle. Your stomach will be better soon. My stomach? Stop. Michelle, for the love of God, stop. Stop? You see there? You see them? More of those goddamn dope pills. That's what they are, fucking dope pills. You're a goddamn drug addict, like your fuckin' father! Well, you will never ever see these again, Michelle! I need them! Give them to me! They help my stomach! The tube is jammed down her throat again and, just as she wretches, darkness bleeds over, and the slow evil rhythms of drum and bass burn between her temples as if she is submerged under water. A dead thumping. But there is comfort there. A warm comfortCOMFORTcomfortCOMFORT.* Shelly struggles to awake, gasping. She is a fish out of water, drowning in air. Her eyes bulge, then shut, then bulge again. The continuing evil rhythms burn in her brain. The seasick feeling eases, but her skin throbs like an infected tooth, right down to the bone. As she rises from the bed, she is stricken by a burning nausea once again, and she can tolerate it no more. Finally, she rolls over and vomits into a metal garbage pail next to her bed. A few involuntary dry heaves follow before she can finally take in a deep breath and refocus...and notice...there are no. Garbage. Bags. Two pools of phlegm-like green bile, mottled with dark spots, swirl at the bottom of the metal can. She stares at it blindly for a few moments, blinks, then painfully peels herself off the mattress and lugs the heavy can down the hall to the bathroom. And in the awful heavy silence of the house, as she quickly shuts the bathroom door behind her with her face in her hands, she hears the high, sweet, evil cackle of a child. She slides down the back of the door, legs sprawling, fingers jamming into her ears to mute the sounds of laughter, as if they exist outside her subjective reality. After a few breaths, the dripping faucet, and the luminous hands of the starfish clock just above the cracked mirror, she refocuses and musters enough strength to reach below the medicine cabinet and grab a bottle of bleach. She dumps about a liter of it into the pail and places it in the bathtub. She rinses it out and the warm water soothes and lures her into drawing a bath for herself. She collapses beside the tub, her head in her hand, too weak to move. So, she envisions it all happening for her. A freestanding, porcelain soaking tub, matte white, appears in the middle of a black marble floor surrounded by colorful flowers of red, purple, and yellow, and eucalyptuses. The shades blend like a Rembrandt. Steam rises off the top of the water. She can smell the lavender Epsom salts. She feels weightless and unbounded by gravity as she drifts to the tub and lowers to the hot water until completely submerged.

I am afraid...

I am afraid to open my eyes.

One eyelid flicks up behind a mask of four fingers.

I wanna keep seein' what I'm seein' and live in that world a little longer, instead of...

A rusting beige tub with spider cracks rematerializing from the drain. Dark mold and sludgy soap scum caked in the crevasses of the broken tiles. She makes circles in the water with her hand and watches the whirlpool twist and twist. *I can't look up! Jonathan grabs her face and tries spreading her eyes open. Yes, look up! So fucking clear, I feel like I can touch the moon! Look. REALLY LOOK! No, I won't look. I have vertigo! I'll spin right off the earth and get sucked up into the sky! She finally opens her eyes, and the stars spiral around the galaxies, broken up in kaleidoscopes.* Her luminous legs swish around in the bath water. She takes a bottle of Pantene and squeezes it all over her thighs, belly, chest, and over her sad, sad blonde hair — sinking deeper into the water to horrify the heavens, maybe a suicide float in the bath. Her head goes down, down, down below until she is completely submerged. Each inch of skin that was once cooled by the air is now warmed by the water. Holding herself below the surface, holding her breath to the bottom of her lungs until she can longer hold it, she floats back up for a gulp of air. A hairy centipede softly crawls along the edge of the tub, moving up the cracked tile, searching. It's antennae feeling the surface. Shelly lowers the bottom of her face just below the surface again, this time without shutting her eyes. She stares so long at the tiled wall that she sees spots. Feeling darkness wash over her, and in the darkness, a face appears, and, though there are no discernable features, a smile slices across the bottom of the face. The jaw becomes unhinged and opens widely, like a King Cobra about to swallow a python. Shelly snaps her eyes shut, trying to blink away the image. A thin layer of salvia forms on the roof of her mouth. She shrieks until her throat cracks and a shooting pain lodges in her vocal cords like a dollop of peanut butter.

Is this what my mind wants to see, or what the mind actually sees?

Sweat seems to cascade from her armpits, down the sides of her pointy ribcage. She blinks her eyes and it takes many seconds for her to clear the evil image out of her head. There is

no hell that can be more horrible and real than right now. *I
should simply not exist. If I slice my wrists, it would hurt too much. I
can picture the pain throbbing in the veins going all the way up my
arms to my neck and throbbing some more, worse than any headache
you can imagine, and there would be no way to stop it. Fuck it all. I
would have to make that decision and stick with it. Not like I can stick
with anything anyway. Fuck my grades, that ugly ass school, and all
the normies who occupy it. They're like a fucking cult. They hide their
pain behind those bright smiles and beauty parlor hairdos and trendy
Gap clothes that make me wanna rip my fuckin' eyes out for seein'
such a fashion tragedy. Hive mentality. If you're not with 'em, you're
nobody. Zero. I see myself in any reflection, really. From my own
puddles of blood to the mirrors I pass to the pale lightness of someone's
eyes, and I see an ugliness that stays with me so long I'll see it during
my next dream, and it'll be that demon I'll be running from, chasing
me up endless staircases that go nowhere. Death finds everyone, so I
thought. But for some reason, it still hasn't found me. I am lonely and
afraid, and I cannot be a part of them and fake it any longer. Walter
told me he made out with a guy once at a rave and cried to me about it
after we smoked an L and shared a 40. I laughed at him, but I really
didn't mean to. He looked at me really sad. For a split second, I actually thought he was gonna yell at me, but he...my chest hurt so fuckin'
much from the inside out after I said it. I judged him. And didn't
wanna be near him after that. I hate myself for it. I judged him. I
judge everyone. I'm like a reptile wrapped in nothing but the scales I
was birthed in, only to bask beneath a heat lamp to feel warm. Living
off insects and larvae. I respond by reaction only. No voice. Sometimes
I don't even do that. I just do whatever it is the body does at that
moment. Without thought. Without reason. Silent of plan. I can never
stick with anything. I fucked up at ballet. I bail out in school when
shit gets tough. My old instructor would yell in my face in front of the
other girls and say I lacked discipline. (What a cunt she was.) I look to
my mother to give it to me, but she fails too. She fails worse than I do*

and that's part of my pain, right there. From one day to the next, until the very end. I am both the victim and the perpetrator. And don't think I came up with that on my own. I heard it right from the mouth of the counselor during a family therapy session after my mom got the shit kicked outta her by her then live-in scumbag of a boyfriend. We had to live in a domestic violence shelter for six months of hell. I felt like a goddamn cockroach, doing whatever I needed to do to survive. I stole food from a local food pantry because the meals at the shelter were God-awful. I lived off ring dings, yodels, pizza, and the occasional dumpster dive. There was a local restaurant that would bag this food that was left over separately from the garbage, and it was usually so fresh! Steaks, chicken, pasta, shrimp...I'd go to the local Goodwill for clothes, but one time I got scabies. They thought it was from the Good-will store, but I thought it was from the roach-infested shelter we were staying at. I was quarantined in this spare room they had in the base-ment of the shelter for like a week. The treatment was pretty bad. The medication burned my skin like a cooling fire that almost made me throw up. I'd put up with that any ol' day over the itching. It was so bad. Imagine the worst itch of your life that actually worsened the deeper you'd go into the itching and scratching, but, at the same time, it was relieving, so you just keep going and going until your skin liter-ally chafes off and you're bleeding like crazy. I know, it's weird and confusing but that's the only way I can explain it and during the night the itching was way, way worse. I actually remember praying to God that I would die in my sleep, so I didn't have to feel tortured ever again. After that, I got really close to one of the psych interns, Bobby. He was the "co-facilitator" of the family and group sessions. One night after a session, we got real close and started talking about all this deep stuff, like God, the universe, destiny, fate, whatever, and I wound up fucking him on the couch in the basement. He was thirty. I was fifteen. He could've gone to jail, but I didn't care. I needed discipline and he gave it to me. Yep. I cheated on Jonathan and never, ever told anyone about it. I felt bad at first, but I don't anymore. I don't think anyone is faithful to anyone in this world, and Jonathan is certainly included. Shelly pulls the plug at the bottom of the tub and watches the grey water funnel down the drain, between her legs, twisting and twisting until she hears the choking, burping sound of the last drops of water being sucked down. She gets up out of the tub, reaches for some hand towels over the toilet, and pats herself dry. Turning from the toilet, she looks in the mirror over the sink. Her eyes readjust under the harsh lights above the mirror, and, once they are accustomed to the light, she can see her face clearly, even the small blemish on her cheek. She leans closer and touches the red spot with a fingertip. The beginning of a pimple. She squeezes it, then lowers her hands. Why bother? It'll just bruise the skin like the others. I'll wait until it comes to a head. If it doesn't just disappear first. Who knows, maybe it will, touching it again with a fingertip. She stops patting the spot, stands back slightly, and just stares at her face, her eyes slowly closing to a squint, her face wrinkling into a frown. She shrugs and turns from the mirror and sits on the edge of the toilet, top down. She knows the room is only dimly lit compared to the daytime when all the lights in the house are lit, but it seems to be just as bright now. What the fuck is happening here? Her mind goes in circles, then blank. She is frozen under the weight of the darkness and the ticking clock. And she waits. For it. To stop. To shatter its way through the mirror to the other side. The. Other. Side. The dark. Sub. Conscious. She cannot resist or run. She just stands there. Hypnotized. Paralyzed. Straining to hear what's on the other side, what's outside the mirror, feeling the pounding of the clock and the drums of evil that burn her brain and numb her soul with a crippling madness. The immobility of time. *I am unaware. Oblivious to the pain and misery in the world right now. Insensitive to the suffering around me. No one knows. They just don't. They seem to think everything is one big fucking game, like making fun of the kid with glasses, or laughing at a handicapped person, or laughing at you when you tell a trusted friend something so personal and revealing (like, they're gay). They just jump around and point their finger and sing, Haha, you're a faggot, you're a queer. They make you cry. They're always doing things like that. And that's exactly what I did to Walter. He never had a chance. And I hurt him by making him feel like he was a kid again, getting bullied. He never had a chance, poor Walter. From foster home to foster home. Most of the families' names he can't even remember. And I made him hurt. Again. He's lucky to be with Stanley and Stan's mom. That's all he has in the whole wide world aside from his art. All those characters he draws all the time, so perfectly and beautifully I can't ever believe it came from his little skinny hands...and that long narrow face...and that bushy hair...those grey eyes that never looked at me the same after that. There were so many times I wanted to say sorry, but it would never come out of my mouth, and when I'd go to say it, he'd just walk away. Like he knew I was gonna say it and didn't want it to happen and he just left. There are always people leaving my life, anyway. They come in and out always coming and going, coming and going without ever saying a proper goodbye. I don't imagine it being like that for me. I don't do the "Irish goodbye". They'll know when I'm leaving. I'll turn around and say I'm headin' for the exit homegirl! Ta-ta for now! Don't wait up!* As she stands there, naked, damp with streaks of water striding down her flesh, staring into the bathroom lights, imagining herself going down an empty school hallway, kicking out the doors, looking up to the sky, and noticing how the sun looks familiar. Her eyes wet with nostalgia.

They say you look like a believer
Look up to see the weakness of the sky
Nobody's out to buy your story
Nobody wants to know your reason why...

6

THE DEATH OF BUFFALO HIGH

At seven o'clock Wednesday morning, Shelly finally feels well enough to drag herself to school. By the time she finishes her tea and lemon cake, she watches the yellow bus stream by her kitchen window. She pounds both fists on the kitchen counter. Mother is not home again, as usual. As FUCKIN' usual, covering yet another shift. She has no control over her staff. That place RUNS her. She needs help. She needs the help from someone stronger than herself. For a moment, Shelly does not think. She looks steadily at her reflection in the kitchen window. Help from who, though? From the devil, answers the voice inside her head that is not her own. The devil is looking after *her*, too, Shelly thinks. And she thinks deeply about this, the weight of fear pulling at her chest, as she walks out the door, preoccupied by her thoughts. Within minutes, she is in mid-stride, halfway to school, and passes a homeless man standing inside a bus terminal. It is cold. He is in a thin Army coat with black, torn jeans and gaunt arms and shoulders, and with a flabby and obese stomach like some monstrous pregnancy. The coat is green and almost new, but it is not fresh. The collar has a tear and flaps in the wind. She is conscious of her line of sight. Peers at him every several strides, feeling his eyes peering at her strongly as if they are laser beams burning the back of her neck. He rubs his stomach as she passes. She feels something evil coming off his body, possibly something inside his stomach. She can hear the wetness sludging around in his guts. Movement. She can almost feel it inside her own stomach. Growing. Living. Pushing its way out. She quickens her stride and cuts through a backyard. As she hops the fence, she sees the top of the Buffalo High. The paranoia. The darkness weighing in her belly, burning her skin. *Don't think about what ya just saw; don't think about it; put it outta ya head, and don't forget ya healing. You're getting better and remember that song mom used ta sing to ya. Frère Jacques. Frère Jacques. Dormez-vous? Dormez-vous? Sonnez les matines, Sonnez les matines. Ding-ding-dong, Ding-ding-dong. Now, keep walking almost there. I can see the football field now and the bleachers. Everything looks tired and grey. My legs still feel like jelly and my head is fucked; at least I stopped puking. Even this walk across the field takes more energy than usual. The wind pushes me, and I pretend I'm floating with it. I Ignore the cold sting of my earlobes, neck, and cheeks. There really isn't anything to do about it but keeping going forward until I reach the school just like there really isn't anything I can do about missing Homeroom, which I will be marked absent. Again. If you miss the first fifteen minutes, that's it. You're considered absent. I've got eight other periods to go through. Four months of it. It's not long when you really think about it, but the winter months make everything seem longer than they really are.*

<Can it be that it was all so simple then?>

The hot air blows in my face as I walk inside the gym from an overhead heating unit. And I pause for a minute. This makes me happy. My face, then my entire body defrosting. I walk along the folded-up bleachers, trying not to distract the gym class from doing their squad thrusts. I don't think anyone noticed me anyway. They rarely ever do. Not even Mr. Grimm batted an eyelash at me. Seems more preoccupied with counting the squad thrusts. 1, 2, 3, 4! 1, 2, 3, 4! Up! Must come up! No slouching!

I still have twenty minutes to kill, so I'll go down the language wing, or, as we call it, The One Twenty-three Hallway, because that's the classroom number of the first class at the very beginning of the hall. And I go to it. And I stare into Madame Marie's class. Before Jonathan transferred to Seaville High School, this was the class I would get him out of so we could go out to the bleachers in the field and get blunted. And that's where I would tell him things that I have not told anyone. Ever. I was scared at first, but after I got it out (and cried a lot) I felt much better. A relief I have never felt before. For someone to be able to provide that relief, to fully listen, comprehend, and truly want the best for me, before and after? It meant a lot. So different than what I'm used to. But we all deserve better. Even those who are hurting and make mistakes because of their hurt.

<Can it be that it was all so simple then?>

Nothing feels real. It's as if today doesn't even exist. And maybe it doesn't. I keep finding myself at random spots around school, outside the cafeteria, in random yet secluded hallways, sitting Indian style and staring at the floor, or gazing out the window from the library. It's so high up there I could see the tops of the trees and my block. Time seems to be going back so quickly, yet slowly at the same time. There are gaps, pieces, of time that are missing. I can't explain it. Wednesday will turn to Thursday. Thursday will turn to Friday, and the next thing I know I'll be at the pizzeria with everyone, not entirely remembering how I got there. Like, last week. I was watching them all in the booth eating their pizza, stealing food from one another, and acting like morons. I feel like I had already lived it. I feel like it was just a movie. Like, I'm watching this great big, long-ass movie of my life and Jonathan is watching it with me. We're just two ghosts floating around, re-watching the movie of our lives over and over. And over.

<Can it be that it was all so simple then?>

The only other time I can remember feeling like this was when I was seven years old during Hurricane Gloria. She attacked us at 145 mph and broke everything I knew apart. I watched her from my back porch. A giant tree from our neighbor's house fell on our fence and crushed the holy statues we had guarding our home. Mom said she didn't believe in God anymore after that. Peoples' houses were split open. Roofs were blown off. Clothes and toys were scattered in the streets. Power lines and trees fell everywhere. Fourteen people died. They were mainly crushed by trees. I heard one family died in their car. It was blown right off the highway. They didn't find the bodies until days later. One was a baby. I wondered what they looked like when they found them. I wondered if any of them were decapitated. We had no lights for over a week. We had to eat and take showers at Grandpa O'Connor's. I barely remember eating anything at all, though. I remember mostly sitting in darkness. Listening to the wind. Waiting for it to get sunny again. None of it felt real. Even when the lights came back on, it was still a dream. I didn't wake up. I mean, maybe I didn't. Maybe I'm still in that dream right now; that's why I still feel like this. Maybe I'm not alive at all.

<Can it be that it was all so simple then?>

I am screaming inside my head to WAKE UP! Strobe lights flash brighter and whiter, and the light rams and slashes her from the overhead LEDs and disco balls, reflecting from the eyes and the teeth of the dancers, their shirt buttons, glittering makeup, visors, glass bottles and bottle caps, and the sheen off the paper flyers lying on the dance floor. *I am here again or was it here I always was and now returning in some twisted vision some nightmare — I need to wake. The. Fuck. Up!* Everything glows and flashes, and Shelly bumps against Jonathan than a few other dancers, but keeps moving, moving, and everything gets brighter, whiter, hotter. *I wanna go home; I just wanna be home.* Shelly clutches a railing and Jonathan holds on to her as they stumble down the stairs to the lower level of the club, the beautiful dark club. She folds herself around him as they move in a maze of slashing strobes between the blacklights glowing around them fluorescent green, white, pink, orange, and yellow. Shelly only sees flickers of wavy smiles, eyes, and strands of light. Jonathan says something she cannot hear. He pauses, then says it again. She stops. Her back against the wall. *I wanna go home!* Folds her arms and slides down. *BACK HOME; back inside.* Her ass hits the floor. *I am scared.* She rests her head on the side of the wall. Cold. Cool. Cooling. Her cheek rubs up and down the wall, and her face is beautifully warm. She cups her hands around her mouth. Inhales the remnants of the Vicks over and over until she can feel the iciness coat her lungs. The cold. Cool. luxurious. Cooling. And she has Jonathan again and the next time, some time, he would kiss her the way he did when he first told her he loved her. And they would go out together. A movie and hold hands or go for walks around the park and watch the waves and he would light her cigarette...Yes, he would cup his hands around the zippo, his cigarette hanging from the corner of his mouth, and I would put my hands around his hand, and he would snap the lighter shut...the cold metal lid. That sound, SNAPPING SHUT.

<Can it be that it was all so simple then?>

But we don't have to go house parties; I know he doesn't like them. I will wear a tight print dress. Something simple. Something slim and neat, but sexy. Not these ugly, baggy jeans. I want him to see my shape other than when sitting naked on my bed in the darkness. Jonathan? Jonathan! Are you with me? Where are you? His head nodding on her shoulder. The shampoo is still fresh coming off his hair. The scent is like the Lavender Fields Sanctuary, rows and rows of flowers...thinking, *We'll go back there this spring, Jonathan.* Her cheek is on the wall. Cold. Oh, my love; I'll go anywhere with you as you will go anywhere I go. A candle. Soft lights of the candle...*No, it's not so cold anymore. Not really. Just*

*like the breeze from the harbor down at Mt. Misery but I want to be
this breeze so badly, now. Just existing, no body, no limitations... pure
as a baby. The slightest ripple on the surface of a body of water. And
seagrass. Yes, blowing seagrass looking at themselves in the water;
nodding, saying yes to us. Peaceful. See, just the slightest ripple on the
surface...hold me, Jonathan. Tighter than you ever held me before. At
the harbor. And a moon...Yes...Look. You see that? It's me and you, all
over again at Mary's Grave, looking out at the water. Oh, how beautiful. I missed it all, somehow. I wasn't paying close enough attention.
How serene. It's Lelah-Jean. The moon follows her. See how it lights
her. Such grace. The shadows will stay, and so will the coldness, but
the moonlight will be the warmth (dance, ballerina, dance like the
good girl you once were; spinning, up on one toe; pirouetting). The
coldness coming on again. The moonlight will be warm and brilliant
again. The tall beach grass, fireflies, flooding light, and the colors burst
and multiply in drops of dew that shimmer and patterns of red,
purple, green, violet, blue, soft pink, and white in the fields of flowers.
Softness. Soft, small round dots of light. Lovely little lights.* I'm cold
again. So cold. Come on, let's go. Let's get outta here now. No,
Jonathan, I won't. Yeah, c'mon! Please? The music. Listen,
Jonathan. The music! You feel it?...it's beautiful. Let it gallop
through your soul. Jonathan turns away and laughs. You sound
ridiculous. Stop. No! It's Gorgeous. Perfect. Look at me! I love
you. Love you, too. Your mouth, it's so warm...*He was with me in
my room that morning! I felt him. Jonathan, can you hear me from
this this dream? I'm in two different places at the same time, I think. I
remember feeling you by me right before my mother barged in and
told me to get up and get to school, I know you were there I can almost
see it again like it's really happening...Do you?* I love you so fuckin'
much I can feel it in my teeth. Okay, okay; ha-ha-ha, I love you
too, Michelle. Now, let's go! Wait! Did you hear me? Did you
hear what I asked you from that other place? Answer me if you
do. Please, just answer me. Jonathan pulls away, angry and

shocked, What the hell are you talkin' about? You know! I know you know! Stop fakin' it! I ain't fakin' shit. Now, c'mon…let's get outta here 'for it's all over, and neither of us will be high anymore. Now, c'mon, let's go! Shelly pulls him in closer, touched by eyelashes. I know you were there. I felt you. I'm not sayin' this because of the E; I'm sayin' this because I truly knew you were there watchin' over me like Maggie is watchin' over you — Jonathan shoves her away, his eyes widening. I know it. I know you know it, too. *I'm watching you back away from my bed, then disappearing and reappearing on the other side of the window* Why…why do you do this to me? My sister…I don't wanna see her or think of her right now. His eyes are heavy with darkness. I just wanna go back home with you…I don't know what you're talkin' about. I really don't, sincerely…And…Stay with me, Jonathan. Keep my hand in yours. Tight. Tighter! I don't wanna hurt you. Do it. Hurt me. But not too much. Squeeze just a little…just enough to feel me. Like, really, really feel me. *It's like one of those dreams where you're flying, and you know it's a dream, but you still imagine it's actually happening, and it's real in that moment. I feel like that right now and I know I can't explain it right. I'm not good at explaining anything, and I think that's pretty obvious.*

<Can it be that it was all so simple then?>

It's like being partly in control or co-piloting a two person aircraft, just soaring through different moments, some I'm reliving, other moments I have never experienced before. Like running home from the train station in the cold all fucked up on E and ending up at my house in my bedroom.

AND MAYBE IT WAS ALL JUST
*A >**dream**<*

7

―――――――

<DREAMS>

Occasionally, time speeds up. Sometimes, it feels like I'm stuck in a particular moment a little too long like right now as I'm telling Jonathan over and over again, I need you to believe me. We're both part of this never-ending thing, and I don't want it to end as sick as that sounds Two silhouettes across from each other. Jonathan traces the naked outline of her body. Rubbing his hands over her hips. I like your hips. They're thin, but wide...strong...I actually...actually, I love your legs. Even though I'm bigger than you, they're longer than mine. I love grabbing your calves... I like your ankles. They're thin but not too skinny. And your feet. The arches; they're, like, really high. And the toes are not so long. And they're always painted and look pretty even though you're wearin' sneakers mosta the time. Shelly leans backward and lifts her legs in the air. Can you eat me out? Jonathan laughs and then rolls over on his belly and stretches his legs out over the edge of the bed. He positions his face over her pelvis, goes deep into her dark blonde hair, and breathes her in, then licks her, tasting what is dripping off her. He goes at her, breathing her in, sucking, licking, nuzzling until her legs shake before collapsing to a corpse. He examines her for a moment, starting at her toes and going all the way to her chin, where the blue TV flicker cuts it in and out of the darkness. Then crawls on top of her and quickly falls asleep, head on her breast. She watches his lips quiver, feels his legs shake, and sees his eyes unfocusing and rolling in the back of his skull. She looks at the picture of Jesus next to her bed and knows he'll never forgive her for this. Her hand grazes along the edges of his dick, bringing her fingers to the tip, tracing circles around the head until the entire area is engorged with blood. His legs kick and spasm. Slowly he becomes conscious of her, the fuzziness of the dream still between the lashes. Her touch, her scent, is this a dream? Am I still in a dream? Is that my hand or hers? The pulsing rhythmic jerk of her head and lips. Her saliva drips down the sides of it, the veins, the shaft. She coughs and chokes and gags, and her eyes roll up to meet his behind half-closed lids. His thighs contract, and a bright tingling surges through his pelvis and groin, and an uncontrollable contraction that sends a semi-painful burst of cum spraying into her mouth. She swallows some and spits out the rest all over his belly. She smacks her palm on his inner thigh, and he jumps from the sharpness of the tight pain. The mark reddens and swells. She glides her hands back up his body, feeling the tiny hairs dragging against her palms until she is bent over him, looking into his face. She lowers on top of him, first with her head on his chest, then drapes the rest of her body over his, then they switch positions, and Jonathan drapes himself over her body, his head on her breast. MTV's 120 Minutes flickering on her television. No talking, just lying there, enjoying the calmness and peacefulness of the room, as if they are each other's sun. Jonathan looks up lovingly at Shelly, I love you. He kisses her on the neck, chin, cheek, nose, and the wet smoothness of her mouth, and then buries his face in her skin and caresses the delicate winglike blades of her back with his hands and inhales her name in her ear, Shelly, Shelly, I love you. She softly moves with the rhythm and absorbs his words and kisses, and feelings flow through her, filtering away all her ruminating thoughts, her fears, and her anxieties, and she lets the warmth flow through her with comfort and vitality. For the first time, she truly feels loved. She feels essential. Jonathan feels alive and significant. He could feel everything from his life that was once broken slowly coming together and creating something new. He is on the verge of becoming an artist of a new reality. Together, they feel complete. United. Though they are still on the bed, they feel a oneness with the stars and the sky and the moon and the sun. They are somehow on the crest of a hill with a gentle breeze blowing Shelly's hair and walking through a sunlit woods and flower-studded field, feeling the freedom of the birds as they fly through the air chirping and singing, and the night is comfortingly warm as the soft, filtered light continues to push the darkness into the shadows as they hold each other and kiss and push each other's darkness into the corner, believing in each other's light, each other's dream. Shelly pushes the hair off Jonathan's face and peers directly through his gaze, I guess we're kindred spirits and that's why we feel so close to each other all the time. *And I hug and squeeze him and the scent of his skin and the cold winter air coming through my open bedroom window takes me back to the after-hours parties we had —*

8

THE EARLY DARK MORNING OF THE AFTER
HOURS...

ut why am I here again? Why this particular moment? Just so my heart can break during certain moments all over again? Why is my mind circling back a few years? We were high at Save the Robots in NYC and continued to get fucked-up all the way home until we got to Stan's. Cassie was in the kitchen making pots of coffee and sucking down sugary snacks. Lelah-Jean, Mackey, and Chris were on top of each other on the couch, lying around like a bunch of lazy house cats, and Stanley and Walter were on separate recliners on opposite sides of the room. Everyone's squished, laughing, sniffing line, doing bumps of K or crystal meth, sneering, each new remark pulling deeper, gut-wrenching laughter out of them. Lelah-Jean was sitting with that bitchy, peevish look on her face, but the boys were having the times of their lives. Not even sure I remember what they were laughing at, but were really digging the crystal, loving the cold chills and chattering jaws as they clinched and ground their teeth and Cassie was glowing...Her eyes beaming...Things were going so well and were tinged with anticipation, but Lelah-Jean was feeling ashamed and tries to relax and laugh it off, but, oh man, that high could be terribly terrifying to withstand, yet she did not want to take the attention off herself, the aloofness that her beauty demanded

— I'm both jealous and infatuated with her — those pale watery eyes, listening, laughing, trying to think of some little anecdote she could tell, some funny little thing that had happened or she had seen... or even something in a movie — Who's seen Symphony? That filthy thing — she's prolly still in the city hoin' the streets. Cassie laughed from the kitchen and added that she goes out there to fuck dudes for dope and sucks the cum outta used condoms for money and all this nonsense that everyone believed at the moment but knew deep down most of it was bullshit. But I do remember the laughter and the feel of every bit of it. Especially when you first held my hand because I never felt happiness like that before. And the lights of candles burning softly and the shadows the jerking flame creates, watching the top soften and the first little drop of wax dribble down the side...blue mixing with yellow...Everyone relaxing and enjoying the flame, the energy of calmness it brings to the room.

Jonathan...I know you can hear this. Please don't give up on me.

9

THE DAUGHTER OF MY SINS

I draw a bath. The water must be hot. Hot. HOT! I feel like I'm battling a never-ending sickness. Where is everyone? Why are they not here? I'm alone in this darkness. You know, you know. Stop making yaself get worked up like this and remember when Mom used to take you on those long summer drives out east, and you'd watch out the window thinking the sun was chasing us. KEEP LOOKIN' OUT THE WINDOW, STARIN' AT THE SUN. Breathe in slow and deep, and it'll all go away like it did last time. Holy Mary, mother of God, pray for us sinners now and at the hour of our death, Amen. Behold the handmaid of the Lord. Be it done unto me according to Thy word. Hail Mary, full of grace, the Lord is with thee; blessed art thou among women, and blessed is the fruit of thy womb. Jesus, Holy Mary, mother of God, pray for us sinners now and at the hour of our death, Amen. Behold the handmaid of the Lord. Be it done unto me according to Thy word. I know if I keep staring at you, Jesus, you're gonna save me. I know you will. I know you will; you can. You're gonna help me.

<Save Me>

My back rips wide open, and the wind blows on my heart, for there are vine-like wings that sprout from the arches of my bony frame and grow like flowers of lavender and pink, and where are my friends? I will gather them together inside of me for every time I see them, I watch their smiles and their eyes, and I think of them as broken. There is a stain on their skin and a hollowness behind their expressions no one else seems to notice, but it all starts happening again, and I'm watching it all like a movie from above circling around myself in the bathroom like a vulture, and I haven't slept for days! FOR DAYS! I'm taking my mother's muscle relaxers to just stop the pain in my joints, my bones, my skin, and the voice telling me, Go. This dark voice. I open the bottle again and again, opening it over and over, and there is a hand that is not mine, shoving the pills down my throat and gagging the white froth and yellow fluid spitting up through my lips. My knees buckle like the floor is caving in, my hands feeling along the walls going to the bath. Now, back to the water, the warmth sliding beneath the surface of the water going back inside back to where it all began, my heart slowing and muscles relaxing and hands unclenching. I am weightless. I. Simply. Slip. Into. A. Dream. I want nothing more than to be nothing. For my thoughts to go blank. At that moment, I wanted nothing more than that.

10

CAN YOU HEAR THE SHADOW GIRL CALLING?

I *need you right now. Can you feel me with you?* It's 1:30 am, and Jonathan finally finishes mopping the kitchen. He twists the mophead in the bucket and watches the sludgy water filled with fish guts swirl around and vanish down the drain. He shoves it over to the corner and gets tipped out by the waitresses and as he slides his red windbreaker over the soiled clothes. He watches Darice count out the last dollar bill of the twenty six bucks he earned last night. She watches him eye fuck her, starting at her high heels and working his way up her well-defined legs to her diamond-shaped hips. Thereya go, ya little shit. All yours. Knock yaself out this weekend. She slaps the money in his palm, and he squeezes his long fingers around her hand, pressing the many rings on her fingers into her bony knuckles. Okay, okay, tough guy; ya can let go now — thanks! She pulls away and see's the hardening protrusion between his legs, nearly poking through the fly of his jeans. She gives a look of disgust at first, but at second glance a smirk forms as quickly as it vanishes. Jonathan faces the parking lot and pushes play on his cassette. He goes home and showers with the song still on repeat, rattling around in his head with some other images.

Mainly fucking Darice. Something else to distract him for the moment. He already masturbated a few times this morning, and he really didn't wanna do that again. So, he just allows the images to happen in random order. Her legs, calves, ankles, neck...her mouth opening. His mouth sucking on her tongue. Her legs spreading; him sucking on the skin of her tightened inner thigh muscles. His face is between her legs, breathing her in. The strong feline odor. He turns the shower handle left and the steam rises. He can barely see the shower head before him. Shelly's face materializes among the haze as if it's bleeding through the condensation from the shower. Her eyes close in on him. The skin on top of his arms tightens to goose pimples. He shuts the water off, dries himself with a towel, and walks through the darkness of a house that's sound asleep to his bedroom. He blindly jabs at a pile of wrinkled clothes from the beanbag next to the television set and pulls a 7 Seconds band t-shirt over his gaunt, pointy shoulders. He slides on a pair of gym shorts and falls on top of his covers, reaches for the remote control, which is stubbornly wedged between his bed and the wall, and flicks on the television. Out of the corner of his eye, he catches a green blinking light from his SkyPager on the desk. Shelly paged him almost an hour ago. *I paged you 143 to tell you I loved you and 911 for help and I saw you smile when you saw my number.* He picks up the portable from his desk and calls her. It rings out over and over. *I need you.* Jonathan switches the phone off and rests it on his chest. He reclines back on his bed, his eyes searching around the room as if he heard something. *Jonathan... please...*He looks to the door. It creaks open slightly. The blackness beyond the door terrifies him, as his face burns with anticipation, unsure if he closed it shut or not. He shuts his eyes and slams a pillow over his face. The coolness from the bright white pillowcase is calming for him. He breathes deeply, over and over, allowing the frustration and anxiety of the workday to dissipate, allowing himself to pass softly into unconsciousness, and — the phone rings. The electronic ringer sends shock waves to his ribs. He quickly answers, Hello? Hey...helloooooo? *Jonathan...can you hear me?* Shelly's voice comes through a thin veil of static. The sound of insects buzzing. Yeah, I hear ya. Where are you? *I dunno...I'm lost...everything is dark.* Jonathan removes the pillow from his face and looks around the room, but it is different. The walls are now bare and suddenly go black. The television flickers to a dull, annoying hum. He feels his legs, his arms, his hands, his breath, though shallow and labored. He feels his entire body, though he cannot move any part of it. Suddenly, her voice rises higher, yet *can you come get me? Please? Jonathan — please! I am so scared...I don't know where I am...hello? Jonathan are you there?* He hears his own breath and nothing else. The room darkens. Shelly's voice rises higher and higher; the sound of insects screaming along with her voice, screaming his name. A tunneling darkness opens before him, and out of the darkness falls one speck of light, and in that light flickers an image of Shelly, *I can see you* and he cannot move. He is frozen. She is screaming back to him for help. A rapid flood of senses surges through his veins, attempting to contain this feeling, using it as strength to move his limbs and exit the state of paralysis. *Wake up; c'mon, man, ya gotta wake up.* Her screaming and the buzzing — THE BUZZING! He forcibly opens one eye and then the other. The room is now half-black. The familiarity of his old room comes to him through the black. *This is a dream; it's all it is it's just a dream.* He suddenly springs bolt upright. Light pools from a flickering lamp. Beyond the open window, the sound of insects slowly fades as he regains focus. The center of his shirt is soiled with sweat. The cold air from the open window hits his face and chest. He shivers in the wetness. After closing the window, he removes the soiled shirt and redresses himself fully. He leaves his room, keeping his eyes semi-shut, holding his hand out, feeling the walls, the railing, and then one soft step at a time. Going downward. A streetlight from a small window above the staircase guides him the rest of the way. Out the front door. Into his car. *I know it's just a dream but I'm following this feeling I have and I'm going to your house to see if you're okay. I feel like I've done this before, though. All of it. But I don't know about this feeling, why I'm feeling it, and why it's coming at me the way it is; I did hear your voice, but I thought it was just me making it up in my head; it felt like I knew the words as they were coming at me, as they were coming at me from your voice. I already knew what you were gonna say and I was gonna say it back to you, but I was too scared.* He drives along the darkening somber roads that always seem lonelier to him in the winter. The anticipation of fear filling his belly with heavy nausea and the perseverating thoughts, asking himself both aloud and in his head why her voice stopped talking to him after the dream —

My hands feel swollen and they're shaking so much it's hard to hold the wheel...

I am so scared...

My eyes can't stay focused on the road...

I am scared...

I'm gonna lose control of the car...

I just wanna feel you with me again because I'm afraid I won't ever —

11

THE WOMB

he calmness before slipping away the heat of the water makes me think of swimming at my aunt's pool floating on my back in the sun and there is no breeze, and I am sinking now, and my chest is caving in, and I have to get out now; it hurts so much it's hard to see or move, and the waviness coming to blindness. Shelly's little house looks lost in the middle of an acre of property. The two dead trees hang like skeletons on both sides of the front yard. Jonathan pulls up and sees the light of the bathroom stubbornly beaming in his eyes. He gets in through the open side door left banging against the molding and finds Shelly submerged to the floor of the tub. He trips over the metal waste basket as he runs to her. White foam and vomit floating on the surface of the water. All he can do is stare, incapacitated by the sight of her.

I am watching you as I am above you

He pulls the drain and watches the water subside, drawing away from her flesh. Dull red patches around her chest, abdomen, and legs. Her lips tinged with blue. Her eyelids half are open. He attempts to revive her, placing both hands at the center of her chest and pushing down. Then, he puts his mouth over hers and blows air into her lungs, only to feel the air blow back into his mouth. *Take me there like you did before; I know you can hear me; I know you remember.* Shaking his head back and forth, not wanting to hear, not wanting to feel the reverberation of her voice in his skull. Her words go over and over and over through his mind as his instincts guide his actions. He slides his hands under her limp body, hooking his arms under hers, then lifts her, his sneakers sliding on the white pills stuck to the tile floor, wet with vomit. He drags her out of the bathroom and into the hall. He hoists her up and cradles her, now realizing how incredibly heavy the dead weight of a human being really is. Her limbs flailing as if they are disjointed. As he reaches the kitchen, the sound of insects buzzing returns. He listens and looks to the window over the sink. Pools of light from a ceiling lamp reflected in the window give Jonathan the sudden illusion there is a shadow of someone else standing behind him as he holds Shelly in his arms. *Go now take me to the car and go-go-go quickly.* An animal growls lowly as he passes the window the sweat building above his brow and the base of his skull dripping down his neck his face flushed with heat the smell of the house like that of kerosine and the dark grey odor of vomit. He carries her in the car toward Brookview Hospital.

Five minutes south of them...

hardly a car on the road...

freezing rain suddenly slanting through the brightly colored traffic lights...

and...

gas stations...

and...

bars...

the hills and gullies...

and...

the car hydroplaning above and down them...

and...

opening a window, a cold chill of madness numbs his soul...

and...

cripples his flesh with angst as he bites down on his index finger...

and...

tears a sheath of skin off the cuticle...

déjà vu becoming him...

he is a moving dream...

It's just a dream, that's all; it is it's just a dream.

The long diminishing scream of the rubber tires against asphalt and the strength of fear lifting her again and carrying her limp and ghostly body through the sliding doors of the emergency room entrance and the fluorescent lights strike his eyes with a dull, nauseating ache. He falls to one knee with Shelly draped over it, stark naked. *The looks on their faces of panic and disgust are worse than how I feel watching them work on you feeling for your pulse, giving you oxygen, and asking me questions I do not know how to answer.* What? Then she took what?! What happened?! I, I tried to carry her, and I dunno. There was a bunch of pills on the floor when I got there, and she was under the water in the bathtub, but I dunno what she did and how she did it; she was just under the water and not breathin'. The nurse, waving her hands and slashing them through the air, I DUNNO! I DUNNO! I DUNNO! SEEMS TO BE THE APPROPRIATE ANSWER THESE DAYS, 'COS NO ONE EVER KNOWS A TING!

Is she gonna die? Is she dead?

The nurse snaps her neck around and shouts, I DON'T KNOW, pushing her shoulders up to her ears. *Fuckin' bitch. Gotta be like that, now, huh?* Shelly is briskly taken away on a gurney. The wheels swivel and spin, her arms and legs bouncing with the sharp movements. Jonathan follows, and a security guard stands in front of him, then shoves him, redirecting him to the waiting area. But he does not fight back. He goes with the guard and, dragging his wet sneakers across the floor, finds an empty seat and lowers himself down on the hard plastic. He stares up at the fluorescent lights, then down at the tops of his sneakers, and puts an arm over his eyes, his mind going and going. *I don't feel much like livin' right now and I don't know how much worse anything can get in my life — truly, I truly feel like that — and I think about when we were younger and everything seemed a lot more fun and brighter especially the summers — especially the summer of '91; drinking from the hose and watching the sprinklers make rainbows on the front lawn and skating empty pools, the Brooklyn Banks, doing whippets and getting high off our asses and laughing till we cried (like when Chris' dumb ass sucked the co2 cartridge the wrong way and it fucked up his lips turning them shits purple and bloody ha-ha), going to Stan's house, waxing up his high curb so we can skate it or watching horror movies all day into the night. I wanna go back there and really feel the summer again because Stanley's hasn't felt the same since. Kinda like "us". We haven't felt the same since. When I first looked at your face, I couldn't stop starin' 'cos I saw somethin' I never felt before in your eyes, and it's hard to say all this when we're together, but I know you somehow felt it like maybe we're connected in a different way that cannot be explained the same way other people who fall in love explain it, but it's hard to say and tell you, though I know you feel it. I just want everything to go backward two summers and stay there a little while longer and hold on to you a little while longer 'cos I really don't know what I'd do if you were not to be here anymore—*

Jonathan lifts his head from the crease of his arm. His face is impassive. Tears dribbling down to his neck. *You're the only person I can talk to about things I can talk to no one else about. You're someone who sees everything. You're someone who sees me.*

12

———

THE CRUEL WIND OF MADNESS

Fragments of images come back to me in a random, chaotic order. One minute I am morphing into air, going back down my old block, playing with my friends, and blowing through everyone. The next moment, I am back in the body experiencing pain. The nurse shocks her heart and revives her; she snakes a tube down her throat and empties her stomach. Shelly gags on the tube, flailing her arms and pulling at the tube going down her throat. HERE SHE GOES! Hold her down! Get her hands! Her wrists! — HER WRISTS! WE NEED SOME HELP OVER HERE! Honey, listen to me…listen! You. Have. To. Keep. This. In. Everything is gonna be okay, alright? Okay? You're at Brookview Hospital — Shelly arches her back and kicks her legs hard. They grab her ankles and hold them. Her body bounces off the gurney and nearly falls to the floor *Why would I try and commit suicide if I was not filled with Xanax? If my body was not already fucked-up from all the drugs I did before that. Why? It was the pain that I wanted to stop. It was the messed-up feeling that would just keep coming and going. It was literal torture. It was like re-experiencing the high over and over again, and no one knew how to help me.* The doctor turns to the nurse and asks her, What's her name again?! Nurse! What. is. This. Patients. Name. Again?! Michelle! It's Michelle. Another nurse cuts in and takes over. Michelle, that's actually my name. It's gonna be okay. You're at Brookville Hospital right now and you're *doin' okay. They just need me to hold still as you take the tube out of my throat and then that's when* the nurse tilts Shelly's head to the side. Vomit spills out into the metal basin. It's okay, let it out. See? You're gonna be fine. Doya feel the need to go again? We got the basin right here. Shelly whimpers and pants and breathes. I want...I want my ma....My mommy...can ya get her...Her face is still in the basin. Wet strings of white/blonde hair hang, dipping into the vomit and sticking to the sides of her face.

13

―――――

REIMAGINING THE PAST

How am I experiencing something that didn't actually happen? Tell me about that one. I see a psychiatric hospital. I am in the psychiatric hospital. Everything is so... vivid. I can smell it, I can see it, I can taste it. I can see the twisted faces screaming in pain. I can even hear a roommate talking shit, speaking the proverbs of the institution, *You don't hear; you listen. You don't look; you see.* But yet, I've never actually been inside one. I mean, we would mess around at the old Kings Point Asylum. We would take the train there, me and the boys, and spray graffiti on the run-down buildings and throw rocks at the windows until we got chased outta there by the cops, and that's how Troy got that razor scar down his face — one of the cops got at him really good with a Billie club, but...anyways, I don't believe I was actually ever inside one. Like a real living asylum. So, where I am right now? I wouldn't say I'm in an asylum, but of one. It's a world of nothingness, yet I have these moments where I can see everything unfolding beneath like a fucking movie. Nah, it's more like a dream. Got the movement of a dream. Only way I can explain it. Just like you said, Jonathan, it's nothing but a dream. And I sometimes believe I can make this dream whatever I want (but sometimes it goes the other way) I'll think up all sorts of *scenarios just to preoccupy my time. Like, if my mother actually did bring me to a psychiatrist, what would the conversation look like? Well, I'll tell you this, confessing only the sins I want to confess. I was so hungry and without food for days on end that I scratched the sides of my face until I broke my nails on the skin and tasted the iron of my blood dripping into my mouth that I got to the point where I hit up Symphony (who was from the same fucked-up reality as me) and started going to Queens to prostitute ourselves, making sure we were so far away from our area we would never run into anyone we knew. And we didn't. But we had this buddy system where we'd always be watching each other's back and never leave the other out there too long. And I see this therapist listening to me, leaning in — some old ass wrinkly dude with white hair who hasn't gotten it up in probably twenty years — listening real good to the spilling of my guts about this shit I never spoke about to ANY-MUTHAFUCKING-ONE EVER AT ALL. And yeah, shit got real. Symphony got her front teeth busted by some foreigner who couldn't speak English. But her teeth didn't break at the root, so the dentist was able to save them with bonding or some shit like that. She told her mom she was trying to skateboard and fell off and smashed her face on the curb. And she bought it. Whatever. And I got it bad myself on one occasion. This dirtbag held my nose while he choked me on his dick, and I wound up puking all over it, and he got off on that shit, too, pushing my face down further and fucking it over and over as I got to taste my own vomit up and down that awful dick of his. It brought me back to five years old when this neighbor of mine, this fat middle-aged guy who drove a truck, came over when my mom wasn't home and made me lick the tip of his cock. It was sticky and smelled terrible, and that's all I remember. I was disgusted with myself, even at that age. I knew something was terribly wrong and never said a word about it because I didn't want to cause any trouble. I don't think it happened again, though I do remember having nightmares about him holding me down on my bed telling me he'd kill my mother if I said anything to her about it. Every nightmare I had of him was the same — pitch black, couldn't see a fucking thing, and I'd be sinking into my bed, paralyzed, and he'd appear out of the darkness, just his face, and it was eviler than it was in person and when he spoke it wasn't his voice. Instead, it was this growl. I was so fucked-up over it I'd wake up crying and screaming, calling out for my mother. And sometimes she wasn't there, ya know, she'd be working overnights or whatever, and I'd be there all alone, drenched in sweat, talking myself down, putting the rosary beads around my neck, praying to Jesus to save my soul. And I watch my flashbacked childhood slowly dissolve as the therapist re-appears right before me, and he comes back softly and slightly different looking, with darker, not-so-grey hair and a little younger, and asks things about my dad and what my relationship was like with him, and I make shit up about my dad — the dad I never met. I'd create this typical scene pieced together from school documentaries and movies I've watched, things I've read in magazines that really made an impression on me, or stories I heard from the group home boys (and that's a whole other story with them fuckups who used to cut the heads off wild bunnies and baby deers and leave them in the trails behind the UA movie theater), and I got so fucked up about that when I saw it with Mackey and Jonathan one day, I had a breakdown and sat in my room for a few days. I don't remember eating or sleeping or who I talked to (if anyone). It really fucked me up that people could do this sorta stuff and be okay with it. And the boys thought they were badass and tough to talk about decapitated animals — most of them are fake about it anyway because I can see it in their eyes and in their souls, they were fucked up about seeing it just like I was. They make everything ugly and things that are truly ugly they'll try and find some sorta beauty in it. I don't find beauty in much these days, but certainly not that shit. I find beauty in movies because they get to create whatever they want and make that world beautiful if they want. Everything nowadays is a cliché. I can't stand a lot of the movies I see. I used to go to the library and take out the old silent movies that had Clara Bow in them and hoped if I watched them enough, her talent and beauty would seep into my soul and change me somehow, and I would maybe end up like her. I would put them on before bed and hoped they would do it during my sleep. My favorite movie of hers is Plastic Age, where she's this popular girl parting all the time and getting fucked up, having fun, and ends in some love triangle. There's something about her that I love so much that I actually wanted to become her at one point in my life. I even went to a past-life psychic hoping she'd say I was Clara reincarnated. And this is just a distraction from thinking about where I am and if I am actually here, but of course, you wouldn't understand — how could you if I can't completely understand it myself — how I can exist in one way and be totally aware, then be caught in some dream world where I have no control over anything. Like now, I'm watching my body*

falling

through darkness

convulsing, heaving, screaming Screaming! my eyes — dull grey, a cloudy nothingness...And the blood—Blood! — I see it everywhere. Dripping from my nose, mouth, and eyes. The darkness opens wide, exposing pillars of white dust leading to a galaxy of milky stars and planets, gushing with blood, pouring down upon me and shooting out of me. I am pushing something out as if it's tearing me in half. And finally. Finally, after it all, the bleeding stops — I find myself in the room again. Cold. Alone. I want my old self back. Want to feel my skin, my hair, my mouth...instead, I am a watcher, existing as air, feeling a sense of judgment and punishment coming from something I can't understand. I feel a sense of something much stronger, like supremely great watching me, but not attempting to talk or communicate at all. Just watching me as I am watching myself lying there. One bed. One pillow. A stiff sheet. An itchy blanket on top of the sheet. One window. Dark blue walls. A cold black and white checkered floor. All ligatures removed, as I heard someone say (probably a nurse) No beeper. No headphones or Discman. No wires at all. They are forbid-

den. No sneakers. No laces. No drawstring waistband. Just elastic. Ugly brown paper slippers. A gown snapped from the back. They don't want anyone hanging themselves or choking themselves out.... like Maggie. Even now when I say her name, I feel a tremendous sense of sadness and hurt. I can see it happening right now. I can see her pulling her head down on the doorknob as the shoelace is knotted around her neck. I can see her doing it over and over — the tears shooting from her eyes and phlegm hanging from her mouth —until she finally loses consciousness. I watch every bit of life evaporate from her tiny body. I wish I could see her right now, but I can't. I haven't found a way. I dunno. Maybe I'm not allowed to find a way. And as her image fades, I'm back in that cold, damp room again, watching myself get up and walk around. Going to the cafeteria, eating a little something. Chicken fingers and fries. Extra salt. Extra pepper. Keeping my head down when I eat like I do at school, not wanting to make eye contact with any of these degenerates. Look at them all, walking around, zoned-out on some heavy medication shit. One woman is talking quietly to herself as she makes tiny pirouettes in place. Another woman sings in Korean. A third walks around carrying a stuffed rabbit attached to a Bible. Another patient is arguing with a hospital aide, saying: I dreamed that the house was burning down, she shouts. D'ya hear me?! BURNING. FUCKING. DOWN! I watch myself get up and go over to the common area where the TV is at. There's a girl sitting next to her on a green leather sofa. Her hair is a mass of tangled red locks, cut short just below her chin. I don't think she's wearing makeup, but her lips are so pink, and her eyelashes are so long it looks like she is. And I get closer and closer to her as if I am going to pass right through her, and with the relaxing feeling of a deep inhale, I am suddenly back inside myself again. I immediately turn and face her. I take another breath. Then another. The calmness of my body. I can feel it again. The second our eyes meet she begins talking. Where do I know you from? You have a really familiar face. Nowhere that I know, I tell her. But there is a strange familiarity about this girl.

I just keep it to myself to avoid any lengthy discussions, because I am just too tired. Not for any other reasons. But I do have that Déjà vu feeling. She studies my face some more, then tells me she'll figure it out later. I look up and notice the TV screen is suddenly much different from before. It's wider and flatter, and it's burning the shit outta my eyes as I stare at it. She is talking excessively and droning on about random topics that are soaring right over my fucking head until I hear her say, Do you believe in witchcraft?

The occult?

*

*

*

*

*

*

*

*

*

*

My mind goes blank for what feels like a few seconds.
Then...
I am in darkness again with little bits of light slashing though the black —

14

THE SEARCH FOR LOST TIME

I'm staring up at these assholes and hating every single one of them right now. I wish the nurse would fasten these restraints so tightly that my blood circulation is cut off and then suffocate me with a pillow as they inject me with a lethal dose of Ativan that finally sends me into a peaceful sleep I have yet to experience. I wish these ugly blue walls would go up in flames and burn everyone in this building alive. Burn the bodies and set them free, what I say. This includes me, of course. I wish to hover over Seaville in an old B-52 plane and bomb the shit outta that dumbass hick town until there is nothing left but ghosts. I hate everyone and everything, but mostly I hate myself. I swear on nothing for no one. I am my own God. But yet, I feel like I have no control. The world dissolves around me again, and I am no longer suffering from the restraints. I am weightless. Lighter than air. I get glimpses of moments, like ruined snapshots of the hated most parts of my life. Faded family photographs of a past I can barely remember. Everything always felt cold and grey and tense and more nauseous the more I think about it. The dark winter mornings at the bus stop. The bright, puke-yellow lights of the high school hallways, that every time I looked into them, I'd get an uneasy feeling that I was trapped, and

I'd never fucking make it out alive. The months blur by. I feel like a stranger in a strange land.

I'm back in a past I don't wanna be at. I'm in Jonathan's room while he's taking a shower and going through his journal. I found a "cute" little note Lelah-Jean left him.

February 11th, 1993: Dear Jonathan, Hey my love. What's goin' down? Nothing interesting for me right now. Yo man, ya know what? <u>I love you a lot.</u> Do me a favor? Let's forget about what happened last night because I understand that you didn't realize what you were doing, so we are going to forget all about it. Jonathan, I love you so much & I am never going to leave you. Never, ever. And pretty soon we will be living together and, soon after that, we will get married. I can't wait to sleep w/ you and wake up w/ you and lie w/ you all the time.

<u>I love you always,</u>

Lelah-Jean

I love you always I love you always I love you always, she wrote to him. I love you always, little cunt-piece-of-shit-whore — oh! I never told you I read that and how I didn't understand what heart-break truly meant until I felt it from reading that note. So, like, I never really truly felt loved before, and I thought I knew what that was when I was with you, and I never questioned it until then. And like a page being torn, I watch that image of myself rip in half as the big fat nurse comes galloping by with a big bright smile, handing out slips of paper with the day's activities to all of us chilling in the common area, trying to be invisible. Some quickly shake their head, putting a hand up as one does when the holy rollers are handing out their Jesus pamphlets at the 7-11 parking lots. Here's the schedule for us to follow, because ya know, we're all just so fucking incompetent we can't possibly do any thinking on our own.

8:30 am: Med pass.

9 am: Breakfast.

9:30 am: TV hour. Common area. There are only 2 remotes.

Return them promptly to the Rec Therapists or SWA (social work assistant) on duty.

10:30 am: Groups (YOU CAN ONLY CHOOSE ONE!) Women's issues (Dr. Patrice Patel, MD). Men's health on Mondays/CBT Wednesdays (Dr. Steven Allen, Ph.D.) DBT/Life skills training (Miranda Johansson, LCSW). Mindfulness/Spirituality (Cheryl Clarke, LCSW-R)

11 am: R&R

12 pm: Lunch.

12:30 pm: Art. Watercolor painting. Creative writing. Coloring.

LAME. Fuck all this shit right now. Fuck Dr. Patel and fuck her Woman's issues bullshit group, where no healing ever happens. Just a bunch of borderlines and depressants triggering each other's "trauma", and I'm there ready to rip my head off and throw It against the goddamn wall. And I am so sick of talking. Words get in the way of feelings. They're not pure. Any time I talk, it's another lie anyway. But, for one hour, here I am, staring at fluorenone lights and pale blue walls. There are no fucking windows, and I fall asleep. It sucks, royally. Occasionally she'll ask for my input. The only way I get through it is by cracking jokes when I can find the opportunity. And there is nothing I have to say. I'm to the point where I just say I'm cured, okay? I'm not gonna kill myself. Can you graduate me now? I wanna go home. The best part of my day is going to sleep. The worst part is waking up. Take last night for instance. Of course, last night's vibe was so fucking morbid it's literally incomparable to last week's tragedy when Debbie freaked out and stabbed Judy's fleshy cyst — or whatever the hell that thing is growing out of the top of her head. She just started screaming, I can't look at it anymore! Then, she stabbed it with a pencil. So, anyway, about last night. During the evening med pass, ol' Sally swiped the rubbing alcohol from the nurse's station and took it back to the waiting room, sat down, and opened it up. I'm like, What the fuck? Then, at the other end of the hall, two older bitches are in a scratch fight (over God-knows-what), and one rips the hair weave off the other's head, and they topple to the ground with a thud, then when I look back to Sally, she's in the middle of pouring the entire bottle of rubbing alcohol over her fucking head. And I'm in total and utter disbelief. I'm just frozen. And before I could get the words out, she flicks open a lighter, and, POOF, she's up in flames. I'm screaming like crazy and next thing I know, there's two nurses on top of her with these tinfoil blankets, putting her out. I'll never get the stench of burning hair and skin out of my nose. This is how desperate everyone is about getting out of this fucking shit hole. They'll literally set themselves on fire for freedom. But yet, the staff will blame it on our "illness". Maybe that's partly true, but I think if you put anyone in confinement like this and treat them like a bunch of slaves, they're gonna lose their shit anyway. So, if we've technically already "lost it", why would you put us in a place like this? Why would you treat us like animals and expect us to heal? What about showing us something beautiful? Taking us on a trip somewhere like the Bahamas, Bermuda, Jamaica, up-state NY, fucking Florida — the Florida Keys. I couldn't care less at this point, but somewhere peaceful. This place is ugly. There are, like, three layers of hard plastic on the windows, and then iron bars. The sun looks like a brown smudge through them. Just keep forcing them meds down my throat until I get happy which is the very reason why I'm here in the first fucking place. It's moments like this I hold on to because there's a clarity to my thoughts that I think brings me to the present moment. Little bits of me come back and then burn up to ashes the second I realize it, and I'm able to escape here.

Then I'm back again.

Sometimes, it's a few years in the past, and
other times it could be
a few months.

15

THE WEEKEND SUMMER CHORUS OF '91

R ewind the tape of life! I watch them in Stanley's living room. I exist as air, morphing into clouds of smoke being inhaled and exhaled from their lungs as they watch one skate video after the other, and I am back there again with them. Laughing, joking, arguing, yelling, cursing, and pausing the tape on the grossest, most fuckedup parts. I find it to be sick, evil, twisted, and malicious, but they somehow find humor in watching a poor boy choke and vomit on a worm as the skaters follow him around with a video camera, hysterical laughing. Stanley loves this shit. Watching us gag and cover our eyes puts a big giant, gapping smile on his thin lips. Luckily, his mom would come through and smooth things out. I had never seen a group of kids so scared of a plastic, yellow wiffleball bat before. She used it often and swatted the shit out of them when they'd step out of line or harass us girls to the point of tears. She'd grab that thing and whack them right on the side of the fleshiest part of their arms or legs. You'd hear that SMACK echo and everyone oohing and aahing, and when no one was paying attention, I'd scoot closer and closer to Jonathan so our knees would touch, and I'd slide his hand down on my inner thigh. We'd all wait for Stan's mom to go upstairs and go to bed, then we'd have Victor smoke us out. On some nights, *we'd go down to 40 Acre Woods, start a bonfire, and watch the flames dance, hypnotizing us one by one. At thirteen years old, there really wasn't anything else to do. If where we needed to go wasn't within walking or skating distance, we had to rely on our parents or the bus. Some nights Stanley's house got stale, so we went to the woods and got blazed off our asses. I know you feel this memory, too, Jonathan. You were the first to leave to meet up with Victor. I wasn't "with you" yet, so to speak. We were messing around, but it wasn't official. I know you were with her that night. I know that's the real reason you left us. That cunt, Lelah-Jean. I like her and hate her at the same time. Mostly all the time. And I know you can hear me. I know you can hear my voice...*

16

———————

APRIL IS THE CRUELEST

Jonathan finishes vomiting, and all the streetlights stab, slashing, skewering his eyeballs as he glances at the puked up Old English with chards of food particulates swimming in the foam. A long line of club kids, skaters, and ravers stand before the clubs' entrance, watching Jonathan. Watching him heave and wretch on all fours like a dog. Some laugh. Others turn away in disgust. He feels himself lift off the ground and, though he is now on his feet, sways awkwardly as he attempts to run. Within his own mind, it's as if he's floating, drifting to his car, which is parked directly behind the club. As he reaches for the car door, he falls to his knees again as if an unseen force, much greater than himself and all humanity, picked him up by his hoodie and then smashed him down into the cement. Kneecaps split by the hard gravel and bits of glass. He dry-heaves a couple more times. Strands of saliva and phlegm drip from his mouth and nose. He reaches for the car door handle, lifts up the latch, opens it, drags himself onto the front seat, and reclines back. *Bring you closer to me. This city is just evil, taking you where it wants to and skull fucking you repeatedly. You told me that, remember? Reminds me of those kids from*

Connecticut who tried to skate Washington Square Park with you guys, and y'all treated them like assholes because of where they were from and jacked their boards. But nothing is like the time when you pulled the gun on Bambi and ended him right there. I know you still think he raped your sister. Murder. Jonathan's body shivers. *Murder.* He turns to his side, reaches down the front of his pants, and pulls out a small spiral notepad. *It's all right on these pages. I was sitting next to you, both of us bugging-the-fuck out on acid at the Tunnel. I'm shivering right now thinking about it. Touching your hands. Holding you. A that moment, I couldn't have felt happier. Turn the page. Read it again. I doubt you even read it the first time after you wrote it.*

Murderers row. Jail me up. 4.15.94

I'd be at one with his blood and die in his shine...Can you feel my words? They're real. Fuck my soul; it's real. Follow the trail down the sparrow's tail. I run in circles. I find it. Strobe light of Hell, give me the power to write. If there is a God, hear me. I LOVE YOU. I feel ashamed but quite cool. I'm insensitive and a damn fool. The tongue on my ear is good. I sweat the snake's drool. She's so delicate, so smooth. Help us, God, ride the trip into the sun...Let the ghost gallop swiftly through your soul. My world will conspire. I can't see you. You're fading to a black dot. You're gone... I took you out. The murderer's soul. Ain't no feeling in this body no more. I got nothing for you, lord. Not even these words. It's gibberish. I'm speaking in tongues. D'ya hear me? Jesus never saves if ya turn the cheek.

JONATHAN FEELS the surge of fear — a yearning in his stomach, pulling him out of his body. He goes in and out of blackness but holds perfectly still, barely breathing, for a few seconds before jerking in his seat, nearly fainting as the first euphoric rush assails his bodily system, and he tries to speak while regaining his breath, Ma... Mom... Mommy... *I got you. We're just gonna keep going at it, over and over. You and me. So, lean back. Listen to my voice.* Jonathan's hand releases the notepad. His bluish fingertips pulse with a fading heartbeat before finally stiffening. *Let it guide you; let it guide you; the louder I am, the closer I am to you, so keep going, keep coming closer<closer>*

closer<CLOSER>

<CLOSER>

Shelly appears over him as his body lies ridged and stiff. His lips tinged with blue. Her lips touch them, and she blows her breath into his mouth. The skin. The eyes. The hands. Move. He reaches up and grabs a piece of her bleached hair and the strobe hits her face, blue, red, green, then bright white. Her bright eyes, translucent, reflecting the light — *I believed you with all my heart when you told me you loved me, I just liked the way it looked in your mouth when you said it. Try to remember all the fucked up painful shit that happened between us because that's what's real. That's what counts. God, we were both so fucked up on ecstasy that night, but, oh, so beautiful, too.*

I'm afraid to wake up.

Take me there, Courtney —

"*Every time that I stare into the sun. Angel dust and my dress just comes undone.*"

17

PURE AS A BABY

I miss you so much already.

    I get glimpses of you in what I think is a dream.

    Then I awake, and I'm back here again.

I saw that girl from the common area. The one with the short, curly hair? I'm gonna call her Clara because, to me, she looks like Clara Bow.

She tells me her name, but I can never remember. Everything is always...in a haze when I see her. She's playing with what looks like a video game, her fingers typing away on this magical piece of glass. Distracted. I sense a closeness to her I cannot explain. I can feel her emotions. The sadness falls off her like burned skin.

18

____

NO APOLOGY

Everything is getting smaller. Shrinking. The blue walls go up for miles as I sink down in my bed, suffocated by own my feelings. There is no discharge. This is permanent. I am trapped here forever.

I'm scared I may die in this room.

In fact, I may be dead already.

I keep hearing the nurses in my head saying, This is your lucky day, Shelly. You get to go home. I try to smile, but it's hard when you can't feel a thing. You know you want to smile. You sense a smile forming, but it just never happens.

I make no excuses for my life. I'm exhausted by it all, but I refuse to apologize if and when I see my mother again.

Not even to Jonathan. He is with me in spirit...

...when he finally realizes what's happening to him.

19

———

BEDROOM ROCKERS

here are moments my mind and body won't let go of. No big trip around the world, visiting exotic places. True love is all in the mind, and that's where the experience is. I never felt the warmth of love from my mother or my grandfather. I just figured that's the way it was. A distance between people. Like at school, you don't cross the line with the teacher and hug her for no reason or just because you're in a good mood. Maybe on my birthday or Christmas, I would get hugged and kissed by my mom, but anytime she got me gifts, I would cry. I would cry around everyone else on a family member's birthday, too. I don't understand why happiness brings me pain. How can we put our feelings into words anyway? It's never accurate. There are never enough words to describe an emotion. I can never find the perfect word for anything. So, I just stopped trying. This happened with everything, too. I did ballet for a while. Maybe a few years, but then I began throwing up before recitals. My arms and legs would shake when I would think of being in front of strangers, basically naked in a fucking leotard. I had no tits, no ass, and my nipples were popping out. I hated the feeling so much that I had to stop. I don't really know if I ever loved — actually, forget about loved — liked being a ballerina. It made me feel as if everyone was always watching me and criticizing me like that cunt of an instructor, Celine. Her face always looked like she ate sour grapes. I could never relax around her. How could you feel relaxed and focused around somebody who was always uptight? I would fixate on her reactions, and that became too much of a distraction because it was all I was able to focus on — her ugly faces — so as I'd be practicing Allégro or whatever, I'd fuck-up and fall on my ass and then get yelled at for it. I was always popping and cracking my neck, knuckles, and ankles when I wasn't at practice. I did it to calm down because I always felt anxious. Drove me crazy and it made my joints hurt. I do know the first time I felt calmness and peace was when we'd be lying together after fucking. My room looked differently with you in it. Listening to the orb's adventures beyond the ultraworld. The entire double album. Both sweating from the heat of the day and the ecstasy, dripping from our pores. Just remembering it right now I almost can't breathe, and it feels like clouds are in my chest and brain. Goosebumps prickle the skin up and down my arm. I push myself back to that moment and become fully absorbed by its beauty. Everything feels almost too good to move. Jonathan reaches through the darkness of the room for his Ventolin. Can ya lay back on me? I gotta get enough puffs in so I can breathe a bit better. Shelly lies back on his chest and smells his skin. Ya smell like onion soup or something. This whole room smells like a goddamn soup kitchen for the homeless, I can't stand it. It's ya upper lip, Jonathan laughs and then he gets up, Why don't we take a bath? Shelly smiles. I didn't think you knew how, and they both laugh, and he takes off his pants and boxers and tosses them on the bed as they go into the bathroom. Shelly puts bath salts in the water and they plop in the tub and revel in the smooth, scented water and wash each other slowly, luxuriously as they work the soap into a lather and caress the lather over each other's body, then slowly drip water over each other, floating away the warmth of the afternoon *It's all fuzzy again and I don't know why I let these pleasurable memories suffocate me...my vision is thrown and I'm pulled backward through a hazy vision that cracks through my skull like a migraine—*

Shelly? the adult female voice calls out again. And again.

20

———————

LOOK BEYOND THE ULTRAWORLD

Shelly?

Shelly?Shelly?

Shelly...are you okay?

I'm suddenly in some office that is strangely familiar. The walls *are green. The fish tank is clouded with green. There is one painting of a sad clown holding a red balloon. A black lady sits across from me with a boy haircut. She's staring at me, well, rather, glaring at me like she wants to take that pen she's chewing on and stab me in the head with it like I have Judy's fleshy cyst popping outta my scalp.* Shelly...hello...What's her definition of rape? I DON'T FUCKING KNOW! I don't even fucking know you! Okay, Shelly...take a break? No! Tell me who you are and what you mean! Been through this before, but we'll go through it again. I'm Cheryl, your therapist. I see you weekly. You're in the outpatient facility Western Nassau on the grounds of Kings Point. And you're talking about Lelah-Jean claiming that she was raped. Well...I have no idea...I don't fucking know. You don't know, or you don't WANT TO KNOW? Don't fuck me up, okay? I'm readjusting. Okay...take a breath. Readjust. *Readjust. I'll readjust my foot right up your dirty old hole. I have this urge to take the palm of my hand and smash it repeatedly into the bridge of her nose right now. These urges come at random moments. Sometimes, when someone's talking, I'll just wanna scratch the side of their face or punch them. I never do, but the thought is there, and it really bothers me. I then think of what would happen if I did do it. I think of their individual reactions and how hurt they'd be, and then I cry. Sometimes I laugh, though. Like the nun Marybeth at my old Catholic school. When I'd be getting whacked on the ass with the wooden ruler, I would totally zone out and picture myself grabbing her by the throat and pressing both thumbs into her eyeballs until they splash up with blood. I could've taken any of them out so easily, those feeble old ladies. All they did was beat up defenseless kids. I bet they never even seen dick, experienced dick, had dick smashing deep inside them, sliding down their throat. Yeah, I'm sure they dyke out, though. I could totally see Marybeth being the butch and forcing little ol' sister Elizabeth's face in her nasty ol' hairy snatch. I bet it has wild, long grey hairs. I bet she NEVER shaves. Probably smells like the rotted Sealife that washes up on the beach. And Cheryl's voice interrupts this little moment of reminiscing I'm having with myself and references something I must've said earlier. Wherever I am existing right now, whether in my imagination or in a dream, I am much happier here —* You're making it happen.

What exactly am I making happen? All of it. You're pulling the negative energy into your life and spinning it like a web. You ever hear of a self-fulfilling prophecy? Nope. It's when you *will* something to happen. You meditate on something so much, focusing all your energy on it so that it actually comes true. That's what you're doing. *Maybe she can see into a place that I can't see. Maybe. But if I say anything else, this conversation is just going to spin in circles beyond infinity, so I'll just keep nodding and agreeing until I fall back into my imagination.* You've just told yourself (and me) you're just like everyone else. I want you to remember something. You have more control over your life than you think you do. *It starts happening again...my focus blurs and shakes, and I repeat to myself, You're making it happen.* Cheryl dissolves into fuzzy dots of black and red. *You've told yourself, even though you don't remember.* Some dots pulse yellow before her eyelids snap them clear. *Just like everyone; like everyone, just like you've told yourself; you're making it happen, and just like everyone you're making it*

just like everyone

else's world...

drifting... alone...painfully alone in their private asylums

unaware of how dead they've always been

Fucking pigs. All of them. Twisted. Venal.

Vapid.

Soulless.

I don't even know if these thoughts are mine or if they're based on something I might've seen in a movie or read in a book. I spent hours upon hours upon days reading about other people's lives instead of focusing on my own. It felt so much better to hide.

PART II

ABOUT A BOY

1

LIQUID SHADE

I'm fucked up so bad I can hardly see the words I'm writing. It's called candy-flipping. When you take Acid and ecstasy together. It'll really fuck ya up big time, but the feeling is like none other you'll ever experience in your entire life. Take the euphoric rush of ecstasy and mix it with the best hallucinatory trip you've ever had, and you'll know why we keep coming back for more. Basically, risking our lives for this shit. Going right out there to the edge of death, staring directly into the void. You see, with acid, there's always the possibility of a bad trip, and with some people, that bad trip could really fuck 'em up forever. But when ya mix it with ecstasy, the MDMA in the E stabilizes the acid, making the likelihood of a bad trip zero percent. Mackey told me he read all about MDMA in a medical book or some shit, and it was used in couples therapy back in the 70s and 80s when they stopped fucking. Yep, it helped rebuild their relationships. I'm sure it was given at a lower dosage, but still, back in the day, that shit was legal. They were probably popping it like Pez candies and fucking like rabbits. Shit must've been off the hook. Now, you can only get it through a dealer, and God knows what-the-fuck-else they cut it with. I know the E-pills cut with heroin are called Brooklyn Bombs, or chocolate chips, 'cos they have little brown spots *in the round pill that make them look like mini chocolate chip cookies. The other ones I know of are called Shamrocks, and they're pure MDMA or the closest we got to pure MDMA. These pills have little four-leaf clovers imprinted on them, and, man, when that shit hits your system, it is literally instant bliss. You're reaching the legends of the highest heavens. Any type of touch on your body is an orgasm. I don't know how else to describe it. But, when you see trains of kids giving each other back massages, hand massages, hugging, holding, kissing, and sometimes fucking in the darkest corners of the clubs, or the bathrooms, you know they're Xing their faces off. As of right now, I feel like I'm stuck in a speedy video game watching all these lights bounce around me, and the techno music just keeps getting faster and faster. There are so many kids running around that it makes me dizzy. I'm scared if I stop writing, I'll pass out and die. So, I keep my eyes focused on the page.*

2

LIQUID SHADE II

The dance floor is packed with kids. Many hold flashlights and suck on pacifiers. Mackey faces off with a hooded dancer. A circle forms around them. *I used to love watching these dance battles with ya, Shelly. Most of them sucked, but every so often we'd catch a good one that'd be worth watching. We'd get kids from Queens that'd come down and incorporate breakdancing into the battle, and they were on some next-level shit, man, let me tell ya. Mackey's fun to watch, too, when he's in the mood, but that's rare these days. The scene has become oversaturated with candy ravers and Guido's; it makes me sick. Everything that was once cool is now dead. Why do things have to change? I fucking hate it. Some days, I can still smell you on me.* Lelah-Jean appears beside him. Her lips move, but the music drowns out her voice. She leans in closer, standing on the toes of her Nike's, and asks him, How d'ya feel? Jonathan shrugs as his eyes flip back like he is going to faint. Lelah-Jean slides her arm around his waist and holds him up against the wall. D'ya wanna stay here or come back ta my house? Jonathan shifts his face so his jaw touches her lips and says, I do — but I gotta work a double tomorrow. Lelah-Jean grabs his hand and squeezes his fingers together until they're tipped with red. I really think ya should come back with me. I don't think ya should drive. How about I drive your car back ta my house? Jonathan sways and loses his balance. Lelah-Jean tries to keep him up, but he is hard to contain with his long arms and legs pulling them both in all directions. She grabs his face, looks at his eyes, and holds the gaze until he feels her damp chill clean and stiff upon his round skull. *Sometimes, the days move in excellence, and I know right where I am going, but other days my feelings get the best of me, and I wind up fucking up every chance I get. Today is one of those days that went right into the night. And though there is still part of me that is semi-aware and conscious of how good I feel, there's also the part of me that's playing Russian Roulette and doesn't give a fuck about the outcome. I'm conflicted. I want to go home with Lelah-Jean, but I know it's wrong. I feel like you're watching my every move. I feel like I'm cheating on you. And also, I know if I go home with her, I'll be sucked into that vortex of a bedroom and never make it out. The same goes for Stanley's. Once you plop your ass down on his ratty couch, you're in a time warp. You totally lose your sense of reality as you're stuck watching skate videos, pornos, and horror movies until ya pass out. It can be the brightest summer's day, but inside Lelah-Jean's bedroom or on Stan's couch, it's pitch dark, and time does not exist. And before I know it, I'm in her bed, grinding my jaw like crazy, feeling every bit of the X hitting every part of my body. And we fuck for hours. By the end of it, my dick is raw. She puts on The Doors, and we quickly fall asleep to The End.*

3

HIDING IN NARROW CORNERS

ere, again, at Runaway Bay Books, staring down at the same page of some bestseller everyone's talking about, but I can't seem to get past this first paragraph. It ain't all that great. Same kinda shit I've seen a thousand times in a thousand different books. My mind is in five different places at once, and every-thing seems less alive and fun these days. My time consists of me waiting for the next outlaw party, rave, or club, and who I'm gonna get my drugs from. I haven't been thinking of much else. But you. Actually, I wrote ya a letter. I remember you saying once that words suck, and they can never describe an emotion accurately. I now totally understand what you mean. I just went off in that letter and said a bunch of stupid shit that didn't amount to anything. Most of it prob-ably doesn't make any sense to anyone but you. At the time when I was writing made perfect sense until I read it back to myself. And it was complete shit. I want to move on from this. I need to.

WORDS ARE *nothing in the face of the void.*

4

TIME WASTED IS NEVER TIME RETURNED

I'm in the same seat at Runaway Bay, and I cannot take my eyes off her. I grab between my legs and squeeze at a painful hard-on. A Spanish girl, probably around my age, keeps looking over at me from the fiction section. She is holding the same book as I am. It's hard to explain, but you know when someone is interested in you for real and when they're just fucking around. This time, I'm confused. I think it may be a little of both. But she spoke to me with her eyes. I follow her. We exit the bookstore through the back, and I follow her through the parking lot, through a hole in the fence, and into the woods. She won't let me kiss her. Instead, she turns around and lets me fuck her against a tree. Her pussy is so wet I cum instantly. I only pull halfway out. The rest is inside of her. I immediately yank up my pants and feel my face burn with embarrassment. She notices this and tells me it's okay and not to worry. She asks me if I liked it and I tell her yes, but I find it really hard to look into her eyes. I ask her age. She tells me she's eighteen and a half and her name is Marielle. She's originally from Ecuador, and if I'd like to see her again, I can find her at the Fairview Inn. She says she's only there on Wednesdays and Fridays. I know exactly what she's talking about. It's a nasty ass, rundown motel on the other side of the highway. Just the thought of that place makes me nauseous. She then kisses me on the cheek and tells me I am beautiful to her. No one has ever said that to me before.

5

PIECES OF WHAT SHE USED TO BE

T his clinic smells like B.O. It's making the dull throb in my crotch worse. I fucking hate it. I've been waiting for nearly an hour just to get my test results from last week. I remember after you got outta the hospital, you were coming here to see some therapist lady. You told me she said I was a positive influence in your life and that you should keep talking to me. I found that to be hilarious. I'm anything but positive. You know, I can't even remember her name, and it was only a few months ago. I sat in her office with you that one time and I was really fucked up. I was stuck in a K-hole. Right now, having you with me would make an hour seem like five minutes. I know we'd be cracking up at these bozos in the waiting room. For a minute, I see you appear in the empty seat next to me, and just as a smile forms, you fade. It happens again. As my name is called over the intercom, I see you again as I pass a blonde girl who is about your height and build. Same way of dressing, too. Sadness finds my heart and fills it up with a heaviness that hurts when I breathe.

I somehow make it to section 2, room 4. This place can be so confusing with all the twists and turns, and there's no one to walk you to your room. You're on your own. How fucking ghetto? I hate clinics.

The room is empty and hot. There are no windows. Find it hard to get a deep breath. I wait no more than five minutes, and the nurse comes in and takes my blood pressure. When the cuff inflates, I feel a sharp pain from the center of my chest that wraps around my back. It hurts, but I don't bother mentioning it to her.

As she turns to leave, the doctor comes in, and their shoulders hit. Neither of them makes eye contact or says a word about it. He doesn't look at me either. His back is turned, and he opens a folder and stares at the papers for a minute or two. Then he tells me I am positive for gonorrhea but negative for all other sexually transmitted diseases and that he is going to give me antibiotics. My mind immediately goes to Lelah-Jean. I don't know why, exactly. Then it goes to Marielle. Could've been either of them. Pointless to contemplate it, though. I imagine myself confronting them both and calling them whores, but then again, I'm just as guilty. Like I said, pointless to even contemplate it. Before another thought enters my mind, the doctor is standing next to me with a needle. I take my arm out of my shirt, and he injects me with the antibiotic in my shoulder. I feel a trickle of blood drip down, but I don't look. I feel him put a band-aid over the spot, and just as I hear him walk away, I can feel my heart racing. I tell him, but he says it's anxiety and not to worry. But my throat tightens and hurts. I see his face drop as he turns and looks at me one last time before leaving. And before I know it, I'm injected with something else, and within minutes I can breathe easier, and my throat is less tight. They tell me I had an allergic reaction to the antibiotic, and they gave me Benadryl.

As I get to my car, I can already feel the weight of the day hitting me with everything else I've been thinking about. I slump over my steering wheel and cry for a bit. When I look at myself in the rearview mirror, I notice my eyes are totally fucking bloodshot. And there is still some puffiness around my cheeks and upper lip, but it's not getting any worse, so I guess that's good. I say a short prayer to God that I'll be okay. Which is weird because most days I'm praying to die.

I end up at Seaville Beach, sitting under a tree a few hundred feet *away from the Bay. I listen to children playing and the waves hitting the shore. Reminds me of that John Lennon song my dad used to play. Lennon had written it for his son. I forgot the name of it, but...my dad loved Lennon so much he named me after him. I look at Fire Island way beyond the Bay. I imagine having a big beach house there when I'm older. Maybe I'd be able to sleep better. Right now, I can't.*

Love

dies slow and fucks you every time

6

LOVE DIES SLOWLY AND FUCKS YOU
EVERY TIME

All I can think about is Maggie and you...The Summer Fest is coming up in a few days. I either had you or Maggie with me every year. I'm still going to go, but I'm not sure if I can go sober. I don't wanna be alone.

Everything moves in waves.

It's all a blur.

Nothing is in focus.

7

MOTEL #13

After a heavy night of drinking, I wake up in a daze. I am somehow under the bleachers at the football field of my old high school. The one place I never thought I'd end up again. The school is surrounded by woods. I hear the tops of the trees swaying in the wind. Shhhhhhh. Shhhhhhh. I imagine myself as one of those Cardinals, hopping from branch to branch, talking back and forth to the other birds. Don't got to worry about shit except for getting shot outta the sky by some asshole hunter. That's the only excitement for that bird, I bet. There ain't nothing else getting at 'em. He's just chilling there on that branch, singing his song. And I'm just as bored. Some parts of my memory come back in bits and pieces. Like spotting for the 40 ounce at 7's. Some old slimy dude got it for me but charged me an extra $5, I wanted to take the bottle and crack him over the head with it.

Walking through the field back to my car, I watch the sun rising over the parking lot, burning the fog away. A little bit more of last night flashes in my brain. The motel. Handing some guy at the front desk all the money I made from bussing tables last week. Then, Marielle. Drinking some Tequila with her in the motel room. Her eyes resembled mine. There was a birthmark under the right one, just above her cheek. A picture of Jesus was over the bed. It got dark. The darkness scared me because the room was unfamiliar. We fucked like rabbits for a while, then...I think we watched MTV before everything went black. I remember how pretty she smelled. It cut right through the darkness, and I still smell her off my shirt.

I sit on the curb of the parking lot staring at my car. A terrific headache finally shows up like an unwanted guest at your door that one of your asshole friends brought along unannounced. Speaking of which, I know I have to move on from my friends now. I can't be around them. Any of them. I did this once before when I moved to Seaville my junior year, but I went back to them after I graduated, and here I am, all fucked up again. Thanks fellas. Thanks for nothing. Thanks for everything. But really, thanks for nothing.

That's how I feel right about now.

Totally conflicted.

And hung over.

Like a muthafucka.

A splitting headache like the sun rising over a scorched earth —

8

THE MEMORIES WORST REPOSE

ow do you recapture nostalgia? Pure nostalgia. How do you describe it? You can't. Why couldn't you see that things could change? And the memory knows this; three months later, my memory still believes that back in May, I saw you at Cassie's party, Shelly. You were drunk and acting like a fucking slut. All over Anthony Minelli, trying to make me jealous. That kid is a cunt. Cunts have no brains. I tore you away from him, and he swung at me. I knew that was the last thing that muthafucka was gonna do. So, I knocked him right on his fat ass. I was astounded at how quickly he went down. I forced you to leave with me. I carried you over my shoulder as you clawed away at my face like a cat, screaming how much you hated me. Well, you couldn't have hated me that badly, because by the time we got to the driveway and I put you down, you willingly stumbled into the passenger side of my car. We took off and you drank from a bottle of Tequila as we careened down Sunrise Highway, talking non-stop in a semi-coherent monologue and shouting out every few breaths, Oh, Johnathan let's go, let's go find my father! I was tryin' to be a good boy that night by staying sober and had to force myself to remain calm as you kept trying to grab the wheel from me while you were also swallowing a long swig of tequila, and I narrowly missed sideswiping another car. I kept looking for cop sirens to come flashing up behind us and was tremendously relieved when we screeched to a stop in the parking lot of the Seaport Diner across the street from the Fairview Inn. (I couldn't have imagined at the time that that sleazy motel would have any meaning to me at all.)

I know Mackey and Chris had favored the place to crash when they were fucked up before they switched their allegiance to the Best Western. I guess they felt they were moving up in the world, rolling in the loot from selling bottles of K they were stealing from animal hospitals. Anyway, in the diner, you kept sliding off the booth seat like someone was under the table pulling at your legs. It was funny, yet sad at the same time. I looked at you, your pale eyes half-slanted and fluttering, and couldn't help but feel partly responsible for you turning out like this. A tremendous amount of guilt punches a hole in my chest about glorifying my overdose a month earlier on Good Friday. Sometimes, I believe I actually died, and I'm stuck in this in-between dream that just kinda keeps going and going. But then I think, when you die, your memories die with you, so it's impossible for that to happen. Your mind is just like a cloud, floating in the breeze, open to everything around it. Like I'm watching you in my mind right now thinking of this, remembering the diner...a halo of gold around us as you slurred, We can be the best couple ever. Don't you believe that? You don't, probably, but we could! You even told the waitress that and how we'd have beautiful kids one day. And then muttered something about you meeting our future child while you were locked up at Brookview, and that she looked just like Clara Bow. At that point, I knew I truly lost you.

Even though I laughed when you told me.

9

CUNT.

I would hear many stories about you for the next few months, none of them very nice. The most disturbing story was that you were living with a sleazy Vietnam Vet character, and you had a daily and expensive drug habit of shooting the junk into your veins. I dismissed the stories as bullshit whenever I heard them, but the idea of it nagged at me like a rotted molar. I just didn't understand how all this could happen so fast. It was only months. April to August. I don't get it. I don't think I ever will. Maybe I wasn't meant to.

Another time, I was driving down Montauk Hwy, and I pulled up next to a VW bug. I vaguely see the shape of a girl and a guy passenger. We pulled alongside one another at a red light, and I looked to my right. You were staring back at me quite defiantly, and your dirtbag passenger was stretching around you trying to get a look at me. From the looks of him, it was obvious the stories I had heard were true: he was old and totally fucked-up looking, with long greasy hair and a straggly beard. It was a very uncomfortable moment, and before I could say anything, the light changed, and I just took off. I never told anyone about it, preferring to remember the beautiful pixie blonde who had come to my door to use the phone on that faithful Halloween night.

Please, God, tell me this isn't true.
I wanna go back. I wanna go back to that night we first met.
Grant me that one wish, God.
No hell can be more horrible than right now.

10

I BELIEVE IN…

A few months had passed before I next saw you. I was standing in front of my house when you drove by in your beat-up punch buggy. You stopped to talk, inviting me to come with you to get lunch at McDonald's. You never touched a bite of your meal but did manage to swallow a couple of codeine tablets, washing them down with the Vodka you had in your water bottle. You told me you had gotten rid of the Viet Nam Vet creep and started thinking about applying to colleges. Overall, you were much improved, though you were still strung out on dope.

We watched Hoop-La with Clara Bow as our last movie together. You kept nodding out. I was numb. Dead. We tried fucking, and you stopped midway, saying it hurt too bad, before finally rolling over and going to sleep. I sat beside you, rubbing your back. You were so skinny that it felt as if your spine would poke through your skin. Tiny purple spots dotted your winglike shoulder blades. This wasn't even you. Curled up like a cat, facing the wall. As I got dressed, I thought I saw your eyes open. I then told you if you ever needed anyone to talk to, you could call me. You smiled slightly and made this girly purring sound with your throat. Though I smiled too, my eyes began to cry, but I couldn't feel the tears rolling down my cheek.

My childhood is truly dead.

11

———

THE BEYOND

he next day, you called me around noon, and there was a long pause before you finally said, Hello. You were even more stoned than you had been at yesterday's lunch, sounding euphoric and slurring your words badly. You had many plans for the future and wanted to renew our relationship. Your voice sounded like that night in my car as you once again talked of going to see your father and meeting up at Mary's Grave later on that night. I finally got you to hang up and, as I was going out, the phone rang again. And lo and behold, it was you again, and you were even more stoned than you had been just twenty minutes earlier if that was possible. You had changed your mind about going out but made me promise to call you in the morning to ride out to South Hampton Beach with you.

12

UNE BELLE GLOIRE

I woke around 10 am and reached for the phone to call you, but the portable was dead. I left it off the cradle all night, as usual. My mother came into my room with her knock-knock open bit, never allowing me the chance to grant her permission to enter. She held the other portable in her hand. The grey one with Maggie's Strawberry Shortcake stickers all over the back. Her face was like wood, and her giant grey eyes watery and wavy like the Bay. Her voice was soft and low, and she told me there was someone who needed to speak with me. A woman answered. It was your mother, and I could sense anxiety in her voice. She told me you died. That you wound up in Brooklyn with that Army Vet and overdosed on heroin. She informed me the funeral would be this Friday and last until Sunday. Your mother had hoped you died in your sleep peacefully. She asked me to write you a poem because she knows how much I like to write and read it at your funeral. I told her I did not feel comfortable doing that, but I'd write you a letter and leave it by your side so it can lay with you peacefully, forever. So, this is my letter to you. I'm folding it up and putting it in an envelope never to read it again. I just swallowed a terrific mouthful of poison. I told my mother I was going *to see you. She asked me if I wanted her to go with me and I said, No. Maggie would be coming with me instead.*

Maybe I'll see you later today, or maybe I'll see nothing at all.

13

UNE SAISON EN ENFER— DELIRIUM I (THE LAST
DAYS OF AUGUST)

I didn't wanna go forward, so I went backward and forced a dream about the past that was unpleasant for me. I admitted to something that I've been carryin' around for a year now. And it hurts. So, I let the feeling carry me wherever it flows, weaving recycled bits of me into the fabric of the past all over again. The friends I once knew were ghosts.

The untidy, cluttered den is redolent of a summer day back in '91 when the boys first met. Now, three years later, the nostalgia is rank and heavy in the air mixing with death and drugs. In the fingerprinted windows, the sheer curtains sway faintly in a hot breeze smelling of fresh earth and honey. Upon the dry oak trees with their branches, small oval buds can be seen forming later than usual this year. Stanley pulls the shade shut. Walter rests on the recliner next to the ratty sofa, a drawing pad upon his lap, his once gleaming eyes absent of life, like two corkscrews hollowing out the oak all the way down to the bottom of a dark, mirky wine bottle. Jonathan sits on the sofa in front of the oval wooden table, just six inches above the outworn carpet. The table rattles with clasps and brass hinges as Lelah-Jean places a half-empty glass of lemonade on its surface. She wears a clean white collared blouse. Her pants are dark, faded, and worn. Her shoes look as if they've never been polished, with small dull patches over the toes, especially about the heels, where the polish fades to overlap. She nudges Jonathan's leg with the shoe. He stares at it. She then places her shoe over his ankle and slowly drags it up his leg, pulling the tiny hairs off his shin. Upon the table, facing him and open, lay a leather-bound bible.

Stanley sits beside the table. He wears a long, oversized Polo. Cigarette burns dot the outer edges of the shirttail. The horror movie's splatteringly violent action and gore can't even hold his attention. His eyes close and then snap open, bobbing head caught in rhythms of vicious sleep/wake/sleep/wake cycle.

Lelah-Jean brings the shoe back down and unlaces it. Slow. Then, unlaces the other. She watches Jonathan watching the slayed teenaged-blood spray across the TV screen. She slides her foot out of the shoe. The tips of her toenails are blood-red in contrast to the flour-white skin. She glances at Walter, who is hypnotized by the movie, then at Stanley and watches him sink deeper into slumber. She turns back to Jonathan and places her bare foot upon his knee again. She drags her toes up and down the side of his leg, starting at the knee and ending on the ankle. She hooks her toe under the frayed bottoms of his jeans. Jonathan abruptly rises from his seat. He neither looks up nor speaks. She turns her eyes back on the television and lets her naked foot come softly to the rug. Jonathan passes the television, cutting the flickering images into darkness between his strides. He crosses the living room and pushes a chair topped with magazines and old newspapers out his way. He heads straight through the back door and makes a sharp right into the bathroom. He closes the door. Lelah-Jean glances at Walter, then the sleeping Stanley, and makes her way to the bathroom.

14

DELIRIUM II (THE LAST DAYS OF AUGUST)

Jonathan finishes up and flushes as the door opens. His pants are still halfway around his waist. Lelah-Jean closes the door behind her, hand twisting the crystal knob. Don't, she demands in a soft whisper. Take them back down. Jonathan stands there, his pants collapsed about his feet and his legs revealed beneath his long shirt. He stands slight and erect. When she leans over, a bit shaky and stiff, he does not flinch, nor does a quiver pass over his face. He looks straight ahead with a rapt, calm expression like a monk in a picture. There is a knock on the door; neither of them appears to notice. Lelah-Jean removes her pants while keeping her gaze focused on his widening pupils. The lightness of excitement fills his stomach and washes over his inner thighs and pelvis. The moist warmth of her mouth. He jerks from the hip, and Lelah-Jean pulls her head away. She backs to the sink and lifts herself upon the edge of the damp, cold porcelain. Jonathan removes one leg from his pants and shifts to his left. She extends her leg and flexes the calf muscle by pointing her toes. Jonathan kneels down and stares up at her. She maneuvers her toes to the tips of his lips and opens his mouth with them. She pushes the first two toes over his bottom teeth, waiting until his lips wrap around them. And they do. She pushes her foot deeper into his mouth until she feels him wretch. So, she pushes harder. Go down the middle, she says with a soft whisper. He traces the arch of her foot with the tip of his tongue. Her mouth moistens, and small bits of saliva fall to her chest. He grabs her heel and bites. She demands him to put his hands down on the floor. He does it.

She pulls her foot away and leans over from the sink so that her chest touches her pelvis, sprawling her legs further out to each side. She grabs his face, pulls him up, and folds him into her, peeling away the lips of her cunt with her two fingers, then wrapping herself around him like a python. The serpent doesn't loosen its grip — unable to feel the air around his body, he squirms and goes in mechanically, with slow and steady force, looking straight ahead. The breaths are short and shallow. Her hand drops from his shoulder down to the crease of his arm. Her long thumbnail finds a small open wound on his elbow and digs in. A sharp zing sends pulses up and down his arm. It begins to leak blood. She holds her nail deep in the wound despite him trying to shake her away. Her lips press against his ear, You're not thinkin' of her...right? Her tongue licks his lobe, teeth biting the edges of it, just enough to cause a flinching pain. Jonathan, going faster and with more force, is too focused to respond. Are you gonna cum? He nods, fucking her faster. Soon? Look at me. She tilts his chin up and demands him to cum *right now.* Lelah-Jean juts her pelvis back and takes him out of her. She grabs his dick and squeezes, starting at the base and moving up with the foreskin. The semen covers her knuckles, dripping down the top of her hand, and trickling to her wrists. She raises the wrist to her mouth and traces her tongue along the skin, licking up the cum, then leaning in and licking Jonathan's cheek, lips, then forcing her tongue inside his mouth while holding the back of his head. He stops, feeling a swelling behind his eyes —

how long has it been since he felt it? His trembling hands press down on Lelah-Jean's thighs, then slide off and grab the edges of the porcelain sink. Lelah-Jean's face darkens. Her pale eyes are like two flames dying on a burning wick, smothered by wax, until the very last spark sizzles and goes black. She tries to find his eyes, but only gets the top of his chin and widening throat. Say it. Her soft, demanding tone rasps with the coarseness of a swollen throat.

Jonathan breathes heavily on the side of her neck, inhaling her skin.

Say it...fucking say it, she says. I love you. Say it again! More, more — I fucking love you, he tells her. I love you loving me, so fuckin' much. Now you say it, Jonathan says, shivering and struggling to hold himself up. Lelah-Jean's throat forces a soft moan that whispers, Fuck you. Yes, say it. You tell me now, c'mon! No, she says. Well, why? Because I don't LOVE-love you; that's why. Jonathan steps back, face receding to a long and angular blank shape. Well, fuck you too, he says and turns to the wall and grabs for his jeans, which have hooked his ankles long enough, and yanks them up. You love me enough to cheat on your girl with, she says. Jonathan pauses as he zips his fly. He looks at Lelah-Jean over his shoulder with a kind of feverish annoyance. What about it? What about what? Lelah-Jean says, massaging her calves. Don't be fuckin' dumb, that shit you just said. It's not a secret, she says. Everyone knows...and everyone knows that...Ya also got her pregnant. Jonathan's face tightens, his jawline broadening and his eyes shutting. Lelah-Jean opens her mouth and then stops the words before they come out. Then, she opens her mouth again and says, Whyn't ya just go ahead and tell her? Whyn't ya move outta my fuckin' way? How 'bout that? Whyn't ya answer my fuckin' question first? Why ya always gotta be avoidin'? If you're such a tough guy, whyn't ya go with her when she got the fuckin' abortion, scumbag! *You never told me you got an abortion. I hadda find out from Stanley. He was the one who took you. Why didn't tell me? Just said you were sick and had the flu. You took the at-home pregnancy test and we both looked at it and the lines were blurry. You said you'd go to the doctor and find out for sure. I kept asking you over and over if you were okay, and you kept saying you were fine, and when I'd ask if you got the results back from the doctor, you'd say, Don't worry about it; I'm okay, I promise. And you weren't. I kept checking up on you. I watched you in your room, curled up in a ball, sick. You said you had the flu. Then, there was a knock on your door. Your mom was yelling for you to get up. I got scared and —* Get the fuck outta my way, Lelah-Jean. I'm not gonna ask you again. She stands against the door, arms and legs stretched out like a starfish. Yo, outta my way. I'll give ya to three. You'll give me ta WHAT?! Then, she spits at his eyes. The tension releases as Jonathan grabs at her, and her hands swat him away, scratching at his face and there is no shouting or screaming of any kind. Her nails catch pieces of his neck and cheeks until he cuts through the swatting and clawing and bear hugs her, restraining both arms to her sides. He bites down on her clavicle and her neck, and a dull, pleasurable expression washes over her face as the bite marks track up and down her neck in uneven patterns. Lelah-Jean, peering up through a screen of dampened bangs, calls him a scumbag. A Liar. Jonathan pulls away from her, the blood vessels pulling away from his face and the rosy redness clearing almost instantaneously. When I left Buffalo a year and a half ago, I shoulda stayed gone and stayed the fuck away from you. ALL OF YOU, ACTUALLY. You're all disgusting. Makes me sick that you guys are my friends. They why'd you come back, asshole? No one likes ya anymore anyway! I dunno...maybe it's because I went through so much shit with you guys, it's hard to let go! And everyone always got along and had each other's backs no matter what, and it's just not like that anymore! And there's nothing left and nothing fun about any of it. It's sad, actually. It is fucking SAD! Lelah-Jean watches his face — the dull flicker in his eyes now slowly waning to a blackened wick — and tells him, It's those little bits of childhood that burn your skin like acid, huh? Without another thought, she grabs for the crystal knob, opening the door —

15

DELIRIUM III (THE LAST DAYS OF AUGUST)

I *have lost control and become the damned of the dead who walk the earth, dragging tracks of blood and shit, sweat and semen beneath my boot soles. I won't die, and neither will they. I watch them like a movie as I hover.* Walter squirms; K-holed again. He tries desperately to peel himself off the recliner, but he's helplessly stuck. His ass is glued to the cushion, and his legs are jelly. Hey. Hey, yo. Fuck didya put on, man? He slurs. Stan is in the same physical and vocal state but even more slowed down and fucked up. Fa...Fay...F-Faces...Faces...ah-Death. FACES.OF. DEATH. Walter squints like a cat. Tortured animals? Ya fuckin' put on a movie about animals gettin' mangled when I cannot maneuver my body away from this monstrosity that's on the TV before me? You sick-sick fuck, you. Stan slumps over, a dribble of saliva dangling from his lower lip. A syringe is stuck in the crease of his arm, also dangling as his body continues to slump forward, inch by inch. *I watch myself walking through the living room as Lelah-Jean returns from the bathroom, and sits at the kitchen table, her hair covering her face. She sobs quietly. I watch myself looking them over, remembering the feeling in my stomach tighten and the anxiety crawling through my arms and legs while refocusing on Stanley, that crumpled being wasting away, suddenly moves and looks up at me. I immediately see flashes of his 14-year-old face from 1991, the summer I first met him. Right in front of his house, skating a launch ramp with Walter, wearing a knit beanie on his head despite the terrible humid weather. But now, dying like the rest of them. I remember wondering what it would be like to yank the needle out of his arm and jam it through his jugular, just to end his misery. Though I am in mourning, I cry, I'm scared, and I wish to be in the fresh air again. I wasn't born into this to be a skeleton with no ghost.*

16

DELIRIUM IV (THE LAST DAYS OF AUGUST)

hen you found the note Lelah-Jean left for me in my journal, I watched your spirit break. I hate her. I don't know why the fuck I was friends with her. I really don't. I never liked her, deep down inside. She's just rotten! I fuckin' hate her. I fuckin' hate her goddamn guts. I will never, ever talk to her again, Jonathan! I will never ever like that fuckin' bitch-ass whore. I think I just always wanted to look like her because she's what you like. STOP SAYING THAT. No, Fuck you! I won't! As I heard myself say it, my heart hurt, so I knew it was true. I just didn't wanna say goodbye to you. I didn't wanna let ya go just yet. *My guts are on fire right now, and the drugs are winning. I have a few hours left before I attend your funeral. And I may not make it. I can't hold on to the guilt any longer. I'm remembering the last time I saw Lelah-Jean, too. The girls jumped her after you told them about the letter and the fact I was fucking her behind your back. She wound up in the hospital with a pretty serious concussion. The hospital staff found drugs in her system and immediately notified her parents. They sent her away to rehab in Florida, hoping she could get clean. Before she left for the airport, she hugged me and then looked me right in the face and said, I'm probably never gonna see you again. If I really hurt you that bad, you can always just shut your eyes and forget that you knew me.*

17

DELIRIUM V (THE LAST DAYS OF AUGUST)

 *nd sometimes loneliness is the best comfort.*

18

DELIRIUM VI (THE LAST DAYS OF AUGUST)

The nightmares continue, and it's hard to tell what is actually happening in my life. I feel detached from all human duties and exist as air, following myself as a young boy, running through the field across from my old home. A darkness blots the sun from the sky, descending upon me —

19

DELIRIUM VII (THE LAST DAYS OF AUGUST)

I *need you to find me again. Please! I miss you so badly.*

20

DELIRIUM VIII (THE LAST DAYS OF AUGUST)

I am pulling up to your funeral now. The parking lot is filled with many cars. The nightmares all occurred within minutes and felt as if they stretched on for days. My eyesight is foggy. Every nerve in my body is raw and shaky. Remembering your kisses, hugs, and incense, mixed with X, taking us to a dark heaven where I begged to stay each time we were there.

Maybe after today, I'll disappear in some miraculous way.

PART III

TRIPPING IN THE VOID

1

ALWAYS RETURNING

To go back there for another peak, another glimpse at my awful demise. There's always some glimmer of hope I can change something about it. Maybe live a little longer. Love everyone a little harder (especially you, Jonathan). But when I go back there, all is forgotten irrevocably. The moment is REAL, chaotic, and uncontrollable. It hurts all over again. The pain in my throat, then chest — that sharp shooting ache wrapping around my rib cage to my back. Each intake of breath is like a knife stabbing me repeatedly. And my eyes bulge, attempting to stay awake, as if I'm fighting against the worst tiredness of my life, and finally, there is blackness. But there is peace. And sometimes you remember nothing from the dream. Other times, you don't want the dream to end; it's so beautiful. There are people you never met but feel like you've known for a lifetime, and when you wake, they're gone, and there's a sadness that lingers for a while until it fades with the stars to dawn. As of right now? I can hear the sirens, I can hear the transmissions and the voices talking back and forth to one other, and it's all so cold and sterile. I would cry, but I can't.

HEROIN & BROOKLYN

Decedent at friend's house when she "passed out". Friend dragged Decedent outside onto lawn and performed CPR. When Decedent was unresponsive, friend called 911 from payphone and then left due to outstanding warrants. Paramedics arrived on scene. Advanced cardiac life support was initiated and transported to emergency room, where she was pronounced dead. History of psychiatric hospitalizations. History of drug abuse.

3

BID TIME FAREWELL

I *curl up in a little ball. I breathe the air right back into my own lungs, and I'm waiting for you to watch over me again as I painfully face a cold winter morning. Reset to zero. I fear nothing, for I am my own God, and I will do this with you over and over for as long as Time exists.*

Even though you won't remember any of this after I awake.

And sometimes, neither do I —